SHERLOCK HOLMES
MYSTERY MAGAZINE

VOLUME 1, NUMBER 2   SPRING 2009

I0555455

"WITHOUT A DOUBT, WATSON, WHAT WE HAVE HERE IS
A CRIME OF PASSION FRUIT."

Publisher: *John Betancourt*
Editor: *Marvin Kaye*
Managing Editor: *Steve Segal*

Sherlock Holmes Mystery Magazine is published quarterly by
Wildside Press, LLC. Sample copies: $14.00 (postage paid in the
United States), $22.00 (postage paid elsewhere). Subscriptions: $36.00
per year (4 issues) in the U.S.A., $72.00 per year elsewhere, from:
Wildside Press LLC, Subscription Dept.
9710 Traville Gateway Dr., #234; Rockville MD 20850
An electronic edition is available from Fictionwise.com
www.fictionwise.com.

FROM WATSON'S SCRAPBOOK

MY dear friend Sherlock Holmes, albeit semi-retired, still keeps himself well informed about the huge amount of literary and cinematic adaptations, continuations, dramatizations, and alas, all too often, transgressions upon his name, character, ratiocinative career, and my reportage of those same items. Generally, I ignore them, except to the extent that my attorney still exacts royalties from sundry producers and writers who thus indulge themselves creatively. Holmes, however, eschews referencing them as artists. "More accurately, Watson, one must label most of them perpetrators."

I am pleased to report that his reaction to the premiere issue of *Sherlock Holmes Mystery Magazine* was quite favourable, though it must be recollected that it only contained two Holmesian adventures, my own recounting of his first investigation, that of "The *Gloria Scott*," and Carole Buggé's recounting of "The Strange Case of the Haunted Freighter," a tale that, though I never got around to writing myself, is thoroughly acurate; indeed, I allowed Ms Buggé access to my own notes of the case.

But I am both curious and a bit trepidatious to learn what his reaction might be to this second number of *Sherlock Holmes Mystery Magazine*. He will, of course, approve of the reappearance of my own report of his early inquiries into "The Musgrave Ritual."

Mr. Holmes might perhaps object to another appearance by our colleague and occasional rival, that Yank, Harry Challenge, though the sort of cases his chronicler, M. Ron Goulart, chooses to set in print are not the sort of thing that Holmes involved himself him with, always excepting that nasty business at Baskerville Hall.

He probably will tolerate Matthew Elliott's rendition of the mystery, "A Reputation for Murder," despite the fact that he and I have encountered Ms Hilary Caine on one or two occasions and, while I have found her to be rather attractive, Holmes, I suspect, was a bit put off by her distinctly discernible egomania.

Now Mr. Schweitzer's "Adventure of the Hanoverian Vampires " — ah, that is quite another matter! I, personally, found it rather amusing, but I suspect it will thoroughly irritate Holmes. Indeed, I have noticed that most individuals, no matter how highly developed their apperception of the risible may be, possess a "blind spot," shall we say, when it comes to humour directed at their mode of professional employment.

I expect that at least Holmes will have no objection to the contributions of Mr Newman, and in that I do concur. We were both rather startled, though, to find in the first issue an advice column by our own erstwhile landlady, Mrs Martha Hudson. I suppose today's economy dictated that she seek an additional mode of remuneration, though why, of all possible professional sectors, she would seek that commodity in publishing even baffles Holmes.

In that wise, she has asked me to remind readers to send her letters for her to write replies in her next column. Send such queries by e-mail to: mrshudson@wildsidepress.com.

Well, now, I've had my say for this issue, so I shall turn over the residuum of this column to the Parker College scholar Professor J. Adrian Fillmore (Gad, what a name!)

– John H. Watson, M. D.

MR Kaye, the editor of *Sherlock Holmes Mystery Magazine*, has asked me to comment on the balance on its second issue. Though I suspect this honour *y clept* chiefly derives from the fact that with age he has become something of a slacker, I admit he has on two occasions done a tolerable job of setting down my own Holmesian, and other adventures; we've also done a few anthologies together, with the cooperation of Dr Watson and the brittle acquiescence of Mr Holmes. Thus I take up the task that Mr Kaye ought to have done himself.

Dr Watson has provided his views upon the inclusions in which he and Holmes are involved, directly or otherwise. In addition, this second edition of *Sherlock Holmes Mystery Magazine* offers "Tough as Diamonds," an interesting mystery story by newcomer David Waxman, and a revenge tale, "You

See, But You Forget," by cartoonist-writer and ex-standup comic Marc Bilgrey.

"Max's Cap," a gangster story with a soupçon of the supernatural, is one of the posthumous tales by Jean Paiva, author of the two Tor Books novels *The Last Gamble* and *The Lilith Factor*, which was a nominee for Best First Novel by the Horror Writers of America.

Doing my best to decipher Mr Kaye's crabbèd cuneiform, I see that the Holmesian parody by Kim Newman, which was promised for this issue, will appear in an upcoming issue of *Sherlock Holmes Mystery Magazine*, as will new fiction by Peter King, Gary Lovisi, Roberta Rogow, Stan Trybulski, Paula Volsky, and Mark Wardecker, in addition to return appearances by Marc Bilgrey, Hal Blythe, Bruce Kilstein, and Darrell Schweitzer.

Well, excuse me, I have an appointment elsewhere and I must open my umbrella, so I shall say *au revoir*. . . .

    — J. Adrian Fillmore
    Gadshill Adjunct for English Literature
    Parker College (PA)

Writers: Guidelines are available on the Wildside Press web site:
www.wildsidebooks.com
Please do not send manuscripts to the publisher or they will be returned
unread. All submissions must go to the editor at his New York address.
While all reasonable care will be taken with unsolicited materials, you
should never send out your only copy of a story.

BAKER STREET BROWSINGS

book reviews
by Kim Newman

The Oriental Casebook of Sherlock Holmes (Random House, $23.95) by Ted Riccardi is a linked collection of tales ('nine adventures from the lost years') filling in the same gap as the stories in the Michael Kurland-edited *Sherlock Holmes: The Hidden Years* (reviewed last issue) and Jamyang Norbu's novel *The Mandala of Sherlock Holmes*. We're concerned with the so-called 'Great Hiatus,' the period when the world thought Holmes dead after his struggle with Moriarty in Switzerland. Doyle has him claim to have poked around Tibet during this time; and Riccardi, an academic whose "special interests are the history of India and the cultures of the Himalayas," extends this to include wanderings throughout the sub-continent, sometimes carrying out official missions for brother Mycroft, sometimes chancing across crimes (as detectives on holiday always do) and too often just poking his long nose in. Whereas Kurland presented pastiches and Norbu delivered a genuine novel, this feels more like fan fiction — it's Riccardi's first attempt at writing fiction of any kind and is hampered by a kind of crankiness that makes it often hard-going. Awkwardly, Riccardi insists on staying close to Doyle by having Watson as narrator, though he is present at none of the adventures — which have to be relayed to him by Holmes some years after the events. This multiple distancing from any dramatic meat is emphasised by the typical mystery structure whereby the detective has to listen to various accounts of the puzzle in question or theorise as to what has actually happened, so that the actual nut of story is too often wrapped in layer after layer of 'he said to me.' We do get stabs at often-evoked 'missing adventures' in "The Giant Rat of Sumatra" and "A Singular Affair at Trincomalee," but the most memorable effort is "The Case of the French Savant" in which Holmes doesn't catch a contemporary crook but delves into a historical Nepalese mystery. Apart from plugging continuity, there's no very pressing need for these stories; and the results are rather dry, only occasionally coming to life as Riccardi works one of his enthusiasms into standard mystery business.

The Final Solution (HarperCollins, $16.05), sub-titled *A Story of Detection* (originally published in a slightly different form in the *Paris Review*), is a novella-length, Holmes pastiche by Michael Chabon, author of the outstanding *The Adventures of Kavalier & Clay.* Set towards the end of WWII, it's one of that subset of stories which finds the Great Detective in his dotage but not senile (though occasionally flustered) and tackling one last mystery even as he devotes the greater part of his declining years to bee-keeping. Amusingly, Conan Doyle's casual, offhand remarks about Holmes's retirement pastime have meant subsequent writers being forced to do at least a couple of days' research into apiary in order to flesh out an aspect of Holmes's biography that his creator probably made up on the spot and rarely pondered afterwards. As in H.F. Heard's *A Taste of Honey,* which remains the Holmes-in-retirement effort to beat, there's a coy withholding of the hero's name, or those of any of his associates, and the aged detective is only one thread of a larger design. The murder of a commercial traveller on the Sussex Downs leads to the arrest of the fairly rotten son of a local vicar, who is ethnically unusual for the region. Holmes takes the case at the slightly-resentful invitation of the local police, not to catch the killer but to find a missing parrot owned by a refugee Jewish boy and which is given to spouting strings of numbers in German which some believe constitute vital coded information. It's a mix of the farcical and the melancholy, with some good mystery spadework but little interest in the whodunit angle. Chabon gives us a credible, cranky old Holmes, contemplating the utopian, mostly crime-free (bar the occasional regicide) cities of his hives and contrasting them with a London he has left behind in time as well as mileage, but finally drawn back to sleuthing again. The title is ironic, since this is one of several recent efforts (cf: Stephen King's *The Colorado Kid*) that finally comes to question the whole idea of a solution — the killer is apprehended, the boy reunited with his bird; but big questions remain unanswered and unanswerable; and it is suggested that the tidy wrap-ups of most mysteries merely seek to impose an order on a chaos which can never be dispelled.

A *Slight Trick of the Mind* (Anchor Books, $12.95) by Mitch Cullin, author of *Tideland* (recently filmed by Terry Gilliam), is sub-titled [clears throat] *a novel* and has a certain overlap with *The Final Solution*. Again, we're presented with Sherlock Holmes the elderly beekeeper, and we find him confronted with mysteries which force him to reconsider his attitude to the whole business of solving puzzles. Like a lot of books about very old people, it unfolds out of order as ancient and recent memories bubble up in the mind of its protagonist. In 1947, Holmes is lately returned from a trip to Japan where he has stayed with a fellow apiarist, who has also sought further elucidation of the disappearance, decades earlier, of his diplomat father (who told his family that he had met Holmes, though the detective thinks he has no memory of the man). As he recalls his trip to Japan, with observations on the lately-defeated people and the ruins of Hiroshima, Holmes is also driven to write an account of an apparently trivial case, involving a woman who seems too involved with her armonium lessons, and that took place just before his retirement. Roger, the son of Holmes's current housekeeper, assists Holmes in his bee-keeping, and is drawn to read the serial-like installments of the detective's memoir, though a surprising and tragic turn two-thirds of the way through the book means he never gets to the end of the tale, which has little in common with Doyle's mysteries and gets closer to the tone of that apparently irrelevant passage about the disappearing family man in *The Maltese Falcon*. Cullin ambitiously gets under Holmes's skin, prodding him to question the way his mental processes have estranged him from 'normal' life — the strongest suit of the book is its attitude to solutions, with Holmes deducing the exact circumstances of one accidental death but never sharing his conclusions and putting forward a tentative wrap-up to another mystery that chiefly serves as a comfort to the 'client' though it's clearly supposed to be a convenient invention. A flaw, to this British reader, is that Cullin too often defaults to American words ('pants' for 'trousers,' 'cement' for 'glue') when supposedly writing from inside the consciousness of a Brit who'd never use those expressions. Doyle has Watson speak of his 'well of English' being permanently defiled by Americanisms, which is an excuse for some writers to take greater liberties, but that get-out shouldn't apply to books written in the third person or narratives purportedly penned by the precise sleuth rather than the sloppy doctor. Still, *A Slight Trick of the Mind* has a probing, troubling, melancholy sensibility which makes it a more distinctive, satisfying read than many a straight-ahead 'the game's afoot' pastiche.

Ghosts in Baker Street (Carroll & Graf, $16.95), edited by Martin H. Greenberg, Jon Lellenberg, and Daniel Stashower, is another themed collection, taking as its motto 'no ghosts need apply' (from "The Adventure of the Sussex Vampire") but endeavouring to deliver cases in which Holmes and Watson are involved with the apparent supernatural. Some contributors walk a fine line between providing a rational explanation and leaving the door open a crack for phantoms to creep in; and none — not even Loren D. Estelman, who also contributes an essay about his novels in which Holmes meets Dracula and Dr Jekyll — pitch the sleuth into a full-on ghost story. The mostly-American contributors also tend to set out promising mysteries which get bogged down in infodumps of historical research — into the suffragette movement in Jon L. Breen's "The Adventure of the Librarian's Ghost," Victorian theatrical lore in Carolyn Wheat's "A Scandal in Drury Lane, or The Vampire Trap," squalour and poverty in Colin Bruce's "Death in the East End" (mostly, and effectively, a Watson story — with a wet-blanket Holmes scene at the end), or Irish cultural and political history in Michéal and Clare Breathnach's "The Coole Park Problem." Stashower presents a neat sidelight on *The Hound of the Baskervilles* in "Selden's Tale," which doesn't use Watson as a narrator; but mostly we're on more familiar ground. Also included are several bits of non-fiction — an overview of occult detective stories from Barbara Roden (strong on the older stuff, but oblivious to any activity in the current century), and a set of thoughts on Holmes provided by Caleb Carr (author of *The Alienist*) almost in apology because his own contribution grew into a novel and has been published separately.

The Italian Secretary (Carroll & Graf, $23.95), by Caleb Carr, is that novel. Here, Holmes and Watson are summoned to Scotland by Mycroft (more active than usual) to investigate a couple of deaths at Holyroodhouse, the Royal palace where David Rizzio, Italian Secretary to Mary Queen of Scots, was foully murdered. A haunting, revealed as a sham, is at the heart of the mystery; and again a pile of research clogs up the gears of the plot. Here's a case where one of Doyle's interpolated confessional narratives or discovered historical manuscripts (a device rarely favoured by pasticheurs) would come in handy. Oddly, a pregnant housemaid who figures vitally in the plot is given the name, Allison Mackenzie, which sounds fine and Scots but is also famously the heroine of *Peyton Place,* an association presumably not intended by Carr. Knowing it was intended to be a shorter piece but grew in the writing doesn't do the book any favours, though it's a decent enough yarn when it gets going.

Ask Mrs Hudson

by (Mrs) Martha Hudson

WHENEVER you wish to ask my advice, you may address your inquiry to "Ask Mrs Hudson" at:

MRSHUDSON@WILDSIDEPRESS.COM

Your query may be of a personal or impersonal nature; I am pleased to give advice on any topic whatsoever.

Sincerely,
(Mrs) Martha Hudson

Dear Mrs Hudson,

I have a problem. My mate Nigel won't speak to my girlfriend, because she called him a mealy-mouthed little dung beetle without a brain.

Not only that, but she also glued the sleeves of his rugby jersey together and hung them from the lamp posts in front of his house. When he complained, she stole his underwear at Christmas and strung it up over the town nativity crèche. Now she's taken to spying on him when he leaves his flat, shouting rude remarks when he gets into his car or comes home at night. She even bought a telescope so she can see into his flat through our bedroom window.

The thing is, I quite like my girlfriend and all, but Nigel and I have been together since our days at Eton, and I don't want to risk losing him. What can I do to make peace between the two of them?

Signed,
Hamstrung in Hampton

Dear Hamstrung,

I wouldn't spend too much time trying to make up between these two; obviously, your girlfriend is in love with Nigel. She is also clearly unbalanced. In fact, if I were you I would sell your house quickly and move away from Hampton and leave no forwarding address.

With sympathy,
Mrs Hudson

✗

Dear Mrs Hudson,

I have a dog question for you. My poodle insists on peeing on my husband's best shoes. We tried hiding the shoes, but little Puddles always finds them, drags them out of their hiding place and piddles on them. If we put them up high then she finds his Wellies or something else of his and pees on them. My husband is threatening to poison her and I am very worried. The last time he made a threat like this my neighbor's child disappeared and is still missing.

I've noticed he recently purchased a rather large supply of rat poison, and we don't have any rodents in all at our house. What should I do?

Frightened in Ferncliffe

Dear Frightened,

First of all, shame on you for owning a French breed of dog. You should get something wholesome and thoroughly British like a bulldog or a retriever, or even a terrier. But a poodle! I can't imagine what self-respecting English woman would go to town with a curly-haired little scrap of a dog like that; personally, I'd be ashamed to show my face at my local green grocer if I owned a poodle. Your dog is probably exacting revenge in the sneaky way any French person would — clearly her motivation is political. So getting rid of the dog is the obvious solution.

As for your husband, I would be tempted to ditch him at the same time. I've noticed that poisoning can become a nasty habit, and someone who is comfortable poisoning dogs and children will likely not hesitate to move on to doing away with his spouse, should you displease him in any way. I suggest moving to Hampton — I have reason to believe that a house there will soon become available at a good price.

A votre service,
Mrs Hudson

✗

Dear Mrs Hudson,

I am becoming concerned about my brother-in-law. I mean, I'm as patriotic as the next fellow, but Roger's attachment to the Royal Family goes beyond all rhyme and reason. He not only attends every public function where the Queen makes an appearance, but he has started collecting Royal Family memorabilia. Plates, plaques, mugs, coins — you name it, he collects it. In fact, his collection is so extensive that the local paper has written an article about it, featuring photographs of his "Royal Collection Room." It is growing every day, and now threatens to overtake my sister's house, in fact — he has already filled up the study and now is threatening to move into the guest bedroom. My sister is at her wit's end about it.

The worst part of it is that he's not even English — he's Canadian.

Sincerely,
Worried in Woolich

Dear Worried,

I regret to say that there's nothing you can do — this disease has progressed too far for a cure now. And the fact that he is Canadian makes it irreversible, I'm afraid. I also detect a note of envy in your letter — I feel I should warn you that this malady is contagious. If you find yourself in a shop looking longingly at a bust of the Queen, or a likeness of the Prince Consort, or a nicely framed needle point of the royal crest, move away quickly and do not look back. Once you succumb the first time, I'm afraid there's nothing that can be done for you. I had a distant cousin who suffered from this highly virulent disease (God rest his soul), and he was eventually forced to move out of his house and into his tool shed. (He was Scottish, so more's the pity.) But do heed my warning — be vigilant, and be prepared to take your sister into your own home when her husband makes hers uninhabitable.

Sincerely,
Mrs Hudson

✗

AND now, dear readers, here are a few more recipes from my kitchen in 221 Baker Street. I do hope you like them.

Hot Crab Sandwiches
This was passed down to me by my mother, who was a great cook. Dr Watson is especially fond of them.

1/4 cup crabmeat
1 cup diced sharp cheddar cheese
1/4 cup celery, diced
1/4 cup mayonnaise, homemade or store bought
1 tablespoon onion, finely diced
2 tablespoon pickle relish
3 tablespoons chili sauce

Combine ingredients in a bowl and mix thoroughly. Pile liberally on good homemade bread and bake in a 350–degree oven for twenty minutes. May be frozen and cooked for thirty minutes straight out of the freezer. Excellent with a good bottle of ale or a pint of bitters.

Creamy Broccoli Soup
Here is an excellent recipe for broccoli soup. Sometimes when Mr Holmes comes in late at night, I have a bowl waiting for him.

2 cups water
4 cups chopped fresh broccoli
1 cup chopped celery
1 cup chopped carrots
1/2 cup chopped onion
6 tablespoons butter
6 tablespoons all-purpose flour
3 cups chicken broth, homemade if possible
2 cups milk (mix in some cream if you like it creamier)
1 tablespoon minced fresh parsley
1 teaspoon onion salt
1/2 teaspoon garlic powder
1/2 teaspoon salt

In a Dutch oven or soup kettle, bring water to a boil. Add broccoli, celery and carrots; boil 2–3 minutes. Drain; set vegetables aside. In the same kettle, sauté onion in butter until tender. Stir in flour to form a smooth paste. Gradually add the broth and milk, stirring constantly. Bring to a boil; boil and stir for one minute. Add vegetables and remaining ingredients. Reduce heat; cover and simmer for 30–40 minutes, or until vegetables are tender.

Tuna a la Varenka
This was given to me by a charming American who lived in the wilds of New York State. Wasabi is a Japanese horse radish, very sharp. You may substitute English horseradish, but the Japanese is better.

Tuna steak or tilapia, or whatever fish you like
Homemade flour rub with fresh herbs (optional)
Sesame oil 2 tablespoons
Fresh garlic 1 teaspoon
Fresh ginger 1 teaspoon
Red or green peppers 1 cup

Onion 1 cup
Mango, fresh or canned, 1 cup w/juice
Red pepper flakes
Black pepper
Soy sauce 1/2 teaspoon
Karo syrup 2 tablespoons
Honey 2 tablespoons
Cream sherry 2 tablespoons
Dried orange peel
Dash wasabi

Sauté fish, peppers, & onions in sesame oil; add other ingredients and simmer until done. Do not overcook fish.

IN subsequent issues, I shall provide the following recipes:

• Mrs Hudson's Finnan Haddie Recipe (passed down from my Scottish grandmother)

• Mrs Hudson's Recipe for Bubble and Squeak (a nourishing breakfast for Mr Holmes and Dr Watson — a favourite of theirs on Sunday mornings)

• Mrs Hudson's Curried Lamb Shank (which kept Mr Holmes warm on cold London nights)

• Mrs Hudson's Scotch Eggs (a favourite of Dr Watson's)

✗

Sherlock Holmes on Radio

The Further Adventures of Sherlock Holmes

A Review *by* Carole Buggé

IT is common knowledge among Sherlock Holmes fans that when his creator, Sir Arthur Conan Doyle, exhausted by the hold Holmes had over his life, tried to kill him off by plunging him unceremoniously off a precipice and into the swirling waters of Reichenbach Falls, he was forced — however unwillingly — to resurrect Holmes some three years later. The clamor of a public hungry for more tales of the great detective finally induced Doyle to bring Holmes back to life in "The Adventure of the Empty House."

Holmes had, in a sense, become Doyle's Moriarty — his nemesis, his *bete noire*. The author's own brainchild had assumed a stranglehold on his life — and, anxious to pursue what he regarded as his more "serious" work, Doyle felt there was no alternative but to do the fellow in once and for all. One is inevitably reminded of another great Edwardian master, Sir Arthur Sullivan, who suffered a lifelong frustration that his operatic collaborations with W.S. Gilbert took him away from what he regarded as *his* "serious" work. The irony for both men is, of course, the same: how many readers of this magazine — a subset of Doyle fans if ever there was one — have actually read *The White Company*? And although the music Sir Arthur Sullivan wrote outside of the famed operettas occasionally shows up on classical FM stations, it is not much of a departure from the gracefully melodic airs of *The Mikado* or *H.M.S. Pinafore* — and, lacking Gilbert's witty, satirical lyrics, it strikes us as lilting and lovely, to be sure, but — well, slight. Together, Gilbert and Sullivan were magic. Apart, well . . . they needed each other to complete the other's genius.

One might well say the same of Watson and Holmes. Or even of Conan Doyle and his fictional sleuth. Doyle may have hated Holmes, and dreamed on long winter nights of killing off his greatest creation — but, in the end, he needed Holmes. And perhaps that as much as anything drove the onetime doctor to lure the famous detective to a certain death at the hands of his fictional nemesis, the delightfully unrepentant Professor Moriarty. (I like to play a little quiz game in my fiction classes. While delivering a lecture on the nature of a good antagonist, after telling them roughly how many Holmes stories Doyle penned, I ask the class how many of the stories Moriarty appears in. The answer is inevitably in the double digits — a testament to the impact of the deliciously evil Professor, who, as I'm sure most of you know, appears in only one story, *The Final Problem,* and is occasionally mentioned in passing.)

In fact, though Doyle could not be said to have invented the arch villain (perhaps that honor belongs to Shakespeare; Iago springs to mind, though there are surely other candidates) — Doyle added a level of modernity to him when he gave Moriarty superhuman genius, in addition to the usual qualities of cunning, ambition, and obsessive drive shared by other great fictional villains (Iago, Lady MacBeth, Javert, the Monte Cristo villain).

Happily, readers of our times are no more ready for Holmes to solve his last case than they were in Edwardian times. And so the Master lives on — in novels and stories penned by a wide range of Doyle devotees (for how can you hope to recreate his world if you don't share a deep love for Holmes and Watson?)

Most people are familiar with Basil Rathbone and Nigel Bruce films of the 1930s and '40s, and some readers may have heard the radio recordings from that era with Rathbone and Bruce reprising their film roles.

And there have, of course, been many other film, television, and radio versions of the great detective — some of them treatments of Doyle's own stories, and some of them original stories from new writers (*The Seven Percent Solution, Young Sherlock Holmes, The Secret Life of Sherlock Holmes*, to mention just a few*)*. And probably the most lavish treatment of the original Doyle stories is the gorgeously produced BBC/-Granada Television series of the 1980s, starring Jeremy Brett and Edward Hardwicke — maybe the best Holmes and Watson ever to appear — on film. Brett's fidgety, restless Holmes and Hardwicke's quietly intelligent, noble Watson strike me as both the most personal and most faithful interpretations of Doyle's characters.

The BBC/Grenada series is stunning to look at — one feels that every detail of life in nineteenth century London was researched and lovingly recreated by the production team. But there is something about Conan Doyle's tales of adventure and intrigue that make them especially wonderful as radio drama. London of that time was a noisy city of richly textured sounds — the squawk of street vendors blending with the rattle of wooden cart wheels and the steady clip-clop of horses' hooves on cobblestones, with Big Ben faithfully chiming out the hours in the background.

And now, thanks to Jim French Productions, Holmes lovers can savor the further adventures of Sherlock Holmes and his ever-trusty Watson in a handsomely produced series of radio plays, *Sherlock Holmes Radio Mysteries*. The recordings recreate the same nineteenth century London that Holmes fans have come to love, all in brand-new stories by Jim French himself that capture the essence of Doyle's world beautifully.

I first came across the recordings when the music director of my own show, *Sherlock Holmes: The Musical*, gave them to me as a birthday present. I began listening to them in my cabin at Byrdcliffe Arts Colony in Woodstock, New York, and I was soon hooked. (Our rustic cabins have no television reception, and so radio or tapes are the only source of electronic stimulation.)

For two glorious weeks, I never once missed my cable TV or my usual fix of *Forensic Files*. I had all the crime solving I needed — and in the much more intimate, personal medium of radio! Here were Holmes and Watson, together again, in the old familiar settings, sweeping out into the swirling London fog, their overcoats drawn tightly around them, in search of a Hansom cab, on the heels of the nefarious criminals lurking in London's seedy underworld.

After gorging myself on the sixteen-episode set my friend had given me, I was delighted to see two more CDs awaiting me in the mail upon my return to New York City: *The Further Adventures of Sherlock Holmes*, yet another Jim French production.

The first thing you notice about the recordings is how rich and well-done the production values are. The opening theme is Camille Saint-Saens's *Dance Macabre* — which, with its sliding, spooky opening violin solo of dissonant tritones, sets the mood perfectly (coincidentally, the same music is also the theme of the BBC's mystery series *Jonathan Creek*). The incidental music in the French series, by Michael Lynch, is excellent, and serves to highlight the action and drama of the stories.

I was disappointed to see that the excellent John Gilbert had been replaced by John Patrick Lowrie as Sherlock Holmes in *The Further Adventures of Sherlock Holmes*, but I need not have worried. Lowrie is a wonderful Holmes, and — whether by accident or design — he sounds uncannily like Basil Rathbone. Lawrence Albert is a sensible, stalwart Watson; and many of the guest character actors (including Dennis Bateman, Ellen McLain, and Rick May as Inspector Lestrade) are delightful, ranging from drunken night watchmen to prissy upper class clients.

The actors' English accents are not all uniformly convincing, but it is a minor point, and it would be churlish to point out which performers could use some work in the dialect department. More importantly, the spirit of the original is preserved in the carefully crafted stories and beautifully recreated scenes, often set in aurally interesting locations such as cavernous museums and London alleyways.

The first-person narrative by Dr. Watson, as in the original stories, is effective but never intrusive — most of the action is advanced through scene, action, and dialogue; and most of the stories contain very Doyle-like plot twists. Most of the time the live audiences are not apparent in the recordings, though in one amusing scene in which Holmes gives Mrs. Hudson (the delightful Lee Paasch) an impromptu acting lesson, you can hear giggles from the audience.

The plots are clever and engaging — especially impressive when one considers that each story runs less than thirty minutes. Jim French has been writing radio dramas for over thirty years, which is not surprising, given the quality of the Holmes mysteries. His company is called Imagination Theatre. Visit their website, HTTP://WWW.JIMFRENCHPRODUCTIONS.COM/, and they will tell you that it is "American radio's premiere drama series, now heard coast to coast on well over a hundred radio stations in North America and by satellite on XM Radio."

Out of Seattle, their weekly broadcasts "feature mystery, suspense, fantasy and adventure, produced by Jim French Productions before live audiences on a state-of-the-art recording stage."

The Holmes stories that French has written were authorized by the estate of Dame Jean Conan Doyle, and a BBC host called the show, "One of the four best radio dramas in the English language." To bring them to life, the website tells us, French studied the master's original stories and delved into Victorian history. A visit to the website also offers glimpses of other intriguing mysteries and dramas available from Imagination Theatre: in addition to the Sherlock Holmes stories, there are the adventures of "a former Chicago cop turned hard-luck private detective named Harry Nile." French created the character thirty years ago for a one-time-only broadcast, but audience response was enthusiastic, "and so began 26 years of episodes featuring Phil Harper as Harry, later to be joined by Pat French as his admiring and quirky associate, Murphy.

Harry Nile has developed a large, devoted following, maybe because he's had a hard life — kicked off the Chicago police force, hounded by a dirty cop who was on the take, battling his own gambling addiction, even losing his bride of one year in a gun battle."

Also available on audio tape or CD are other tales of Raffles, which are "based on stories written by E.W. Hornung, the brother-in-law of Holmes's creator Sir Arthur Conan Doyle." Raffles is "that fabulous rogue of Victorian society A.J. Raffles" (played by actor John Armstrong). Some of the stories available are "The Ides of March," "A Costume Piece," and a completely original play by M. J. Elliott "A Gift From the Gods."

There are other delights to be found as well, such as Act One Audio from Topics Entertainment, a collection from the *Movies for Your Mind* series of Jim French mysteries, suspense dramas, Sci-Fi, and fantasy radio shows which first aired over KVI in Seattle in a series called *Crisis*.

So brew yourself a cup of tea (or indulge in something stronger — say, a decent glass of Port), put your feet up, fire up the CD player, and settle in to enjoy a jolly good adventure, courtesy of Jim French and friends!   ✗

The Adventure of the Hanoverian Vampires

by Darrell Schweitzer

I FOUND it. It was mine, a pretty, shiny thing, which I found amusing to swat about on the ground for several minutes, watching the evening sunlight gleam off the polished surface. Then, of course, I lost interest and left it where it lay. But it was still mine. So when one of the "street arabs" — verminous *boys* — snatched it up, I yowled in protest and gave the villain a fine raking on the calf.

He yowled right back and kicked me away. I landed nimbly and hissed, ready for another round of combat.

"What have you got there, Billy?" came another voice.

"I dunno, Mr. 'Olmes."

"I'll give you a shilling for it."

The transaction was done, though the shiny object was still mine.

But now I was content, for the trouser leg I rubbed against belonged to the most perceptive of all human beings, the Great Detective himself, and the result of that encounter is the only Sherlock Holmes adventure ever narrated by a cat.

It is not possible for me to give you my name, for the true names of cats are never revealed outside our secretive tribe, and not even Sherlock Holmes may deduce them; whether the street arabs or Dr. Watson called me Fluffy or Mouser or something far less complimentary is, frankly, beneath notice. Suffice it to say that Holmes and I had a certain understanding by which we recognized and respected one another. You won't read of any of this in the chronicles penned by the doltish Watson, an altogether inferior lump of clay, *who once owned a bulldog pup,* probably without appreciating the crucial distinction that one *owns* a dog but *entertains* a cat. A dog is a useful object, even as, I suppose, Watson at times was useful.

But he tried to shoo me away, hissing, "Scat!" and other ridiculous imprecations, before Holmes drew his attention to the object in hand.

"It is the clue we have been seeking," said he. "Come Watson, we have much to do this night. It would be well if you brought your revolver."

MOMENTS later, all three of us were clattering along the rapidly darkening streets of London in a Hansom. At first the driver, like the boorish Watson, objected to my presence, but Holmes gave the driver an extra coin. Watson, dog-like, acquiesced. Holmes would have found it useless to explain to him that cats partake of the most ancient mysteries of the dark, and so have a proper place in any night of intrigue and adventure.

It was indeed such a night.

As we wove through the narrow, filthy streets of the East End, past increasingly disreputable denizens, Holmes held up the shiny thing — which I now conceded I had *loaned* to Mr. Holmes.

"Deduce, Watson."

I assume this was a game for Holmes, like swatting a ball of string.

"It is a very thin locket," said Watson, "for I see that a spring-lock opens it —"

"Look out, Watson!" cried Holmes, for Watson had unthinkingly sprung open the locket, allowing a scrap of paper to flutter out. Deftly, Holmes snatched the paper out of the air.

"What is it, Holmes?"

"Momentarily, Watson. First, the locket."

"It and its chain are gold-plated."

"Not silver, Watson. Perhaps you will see the significance of that."

Obviously not. Watson continued, "On one side, is a female portrait — not an attractive one, I dare say —"

"I shall entirely trust your judgment in that department, Watson. Pray, continue."

"She wears a royal crown. The inscription is in German, and it reads: VICTORIA KAISERIN GROSS BRITANNIEN — Good God, Holmes!"

"Yes, Watson, it is the emblem of the current Hanoverian pretender, whose plottings against our king and country never cease, even after the failure — so ably chronicled by another writer — of the desperate scheme to place St. Paul's Cathedral on rollers and wheel it into the Thames, back in the days of James the Fourth."

"God save His Majesty, King James the Sixth, and all the House of Stuart!"

"A sentiment I echo, Watson, but we must hurry on and

save the patriotism for our leisure. As you see, we are running out of time."

I placed my paws on the high dashboard of the Hansom for a better view. We were near the London docks. A fog had settled in among the poorly-lit streets. The air was thick with strange smells. Many of the passers-by were foreigners of the most unsavory sort.

"Recall, Watson," said Holmes, "that the notorious Dr. Moriarty, before he turned to crime, wrote, in addition to a curious monograph about an asteroid, a treatise on the possibility of an infinity of alternative worlds existing side by side, which may perhaps be *realized* by the use of certain potent objects — he actually used the word 'numinous' — which suggest all manner of fantastic combinations, such as, for example, one in which Bonnie Prince Charlie was *defeated* at Culloden and England today is ruled by this same unhandsome *Victoria* of the House of Hanover —"

"Good God, Holmes!"

"You could as well imagine a world in which you, Watson, are Grand Panjandrum of Nabobistan, complete with harem. You would enjoy that, would you not?"

"I wouldn't be with you, Holmes," he said with some regret.

For an instant I almost admired Watson, though I knew his was mere dog-like loyalty.

"But to conclude," said Holmes, "it was Moriarty's theory, which I believe he has passed on to his Hanoverian confederates and which will perhaps be put to the test tonight, that with the use of such an object, *which has been manufactured in one of the alternative worlds and conjured into ours,* all manner of what the ignorant would call supernatural beings or creatures may be imposed —"

At that moment the Hansom came to a halt. We three debarked. The cab hurried off. I ran ahead of the two humans, into the gloom. The hideous smell of the river and of river rats was ahead of me.

Holmes and Watson hurried to keep pace with me, their great, clumsy feet thundering on the pavement. Dr. Watson gasped between breaths.

"This theory, Holmes, seems perfectly insane —"

"Watson, at such times it pays to be a little mad!"

"And you, the rationalist!"

Holmes made no reply to Watson's taunt, for we had come to our destination, a deserted wharf amid tumbledown warehouses. The fog was so thick it seemed a solid thing. Even I shivered.

Holmes struck a match for light. He held the paper from inside the locket up so Watson could read it.

"It is a shipping document," said Watson. "In receipt of five boxes of earth . . . what would anybody want with those, Holmes?"

"Observe the crest, Watson."

"An odd one. With a bat —"

"It is the arms of a certain *voivode* of Transylvania, a Count Dracula, about whom many terrible things are whispered. Now all the pieces of the puzzle come together. This Dracula, in the employ of the Hanoverians, under the direction of Moriarty —"

"I don't understand, Holmes."

Impatiently, Holmes got out the locket and showed Watson the reverse.

"It's the same crest, Holmes, to be sure, but —"

I let out a screech of challenge, and at this point Holmes had no time to deal with Watson's thick-headedness. A low, flat barge drifted out of the fog toward the wharf, heavily laden with long, rectangular boxes.

"Quick, Watson! Under no circumstances must that vessel be allowed to touch land!"

THE two of them ran to the end of the wharf, and with a long leap all three of us landed squarely in the middle of the approaching barge. Watson's thick head proved to be of some service at this point, I must admit, because even as we landed one of those disreputable foreigners arose from behind one of the boxes and clubbed Watson with a stout cudgel, which would have broken his skull had it not been so thick, but instead sent him tumbling back against his assailant, who was thus set off balance.

Sherlock Holmes, strikingly agile for a human, had all the advantage he needed. He dealt with the single *live* crewman on the barge, leaving him unconscious at his feet.

But even he could not quite grasp the *true* danger. *I* was the one who first appreciated the significance of the horrible carrion smell which wafted from the boxes, now all the more intense as the lids of those boxes creaked and rose up, *opened from within.*

In the struggle, Holmes dropped the gold locket. It gleamed even in the poor light.

The *thing,* which streaked out of one of the boxes far more swiftly than the other occupant could emerge, went straight for the locket, swatted it to one side, then to the other, then turned to confront me.

"Mine!" I communicated, in the secret language of cats, which no human may ever understand.

When I call it a cat, I use the term loosely, for though it had the form of a huge, black-furred tom, it was a *dead* thing with burning red eyes and glistening fangs. We struggled even as Holmes and his opponents did, both seeking to regain the shiny locket-and-chain, while we rolled right to the edge of the barge's deck, mere inches above the noxious water.

That was when the inspiration came to me, though I paid a terrible price.

I let go of what was *mine*. Instantly my enemy grabbed hold of the chain with both forepaws and became entangled, and it took but a single swipe for me to knock him over the side into the water. The carrion-thing let out a hideous yowl, then *exploded* into steam upon contact with the water and was gone.

As was my pretty treasure.

THE rest is less interesting. Holmes, seeing a variety of carrion *humans* emerging from the wooden boxes, heaved first the barge's anchor, then the semi-conscious Watson and the inert crewman over the side and leapt into the water himself. He stood up, awash to his shoulders. I might have been in a difficult situation had he not allowed me to ride atop his head all the way to shore, while he dragged Watson and the nautical thug.

Once on land, we watched the hideous spectacle of the carrion things stumbling about, seemingly unable to figure any way out of their present predicament.

"The vampires are rendered helpless by the running water of the good Thames," Holmes explained. "So enfeebled, they cannot even raise the anchor. Daylight will force them back into their boxes, where they are easily destroyed."

"What I don't understand," said Watson, the following morning, back in Baker Street, "is how the locket got there in the first place."

While they spoke, I lapped a well-deserved saucer of milk, despite Watson's disapproval.

"I think Count Dracula — who was not among the vampires destroyed, and has yet escaped us — was betrayed by his cat."

Holmes got out *the locket* and dangled it by its chain.

Watson stuttered. Even I looked up in amazement.

Holmes laughed. "When the sun rose and the tide went out, I hired one of the Irregulars to splash around in the shallow water until he found it."

The thought of a "street arab" immersing himself in the nasty element to recover my prize made me think that even boys have their uses.

"Dracula's feline," said Holmes, "must have passed from ship to shore many times, perhaps carried by a human agent, to serve as a scout. On one of those missions, it stole the crucial locket, hen, losing interest, abandoned it. The object is a perfect cat-toy, don't you think?"

He dangled the beautiful thing on its chain. I watched, fascinated. But I continued with my milk. It was *mine,* after all, and I could play with it later.

You See, but You Forget
by Marc Bilgrey

THE instant Hector Nunez knocked on the door he knew that something was wrong. "Mrs. Gonzales?" he said. "It's me, Hector."

There was no answer. Hector tried again, but still got no response. He put his hand on the doorknob and twisted it. It turned. How many times had he told Mrs. Gonzales to lock her door? She would just smile and tell him that he worried too much. Wasn't that what neighbors were supposed to do, worry about each other? Look after each other?

Hector walked into the dark apartment and looked around. Even though he was wearing gloves, he blew on his hands and rubbed them together. Something was definitely wrong. He smelled nothing. Mrs. Gonzales always made hot cocoa for him in the morning.

He should be smelling it, he thought, as he inched his way past a table and a worn chair.

Then he shivered. It was even colder here than his apartment next door.

He peeked into the bedroom and there on the floor was Mrs. Gonzales. He ran over and kneeled down next to her. Her face was to the wall, wrapped in a dirty blanket.

"Mrs. Gonzales?" he said softly. She didn't move.

He took off his right glove and felt her face. It was cold. As cold as the room she was in. He turned her toward him. Her eyes stared at the ceiling, unblinking.

Hector went downstairs and told Mr. Rodriguez, the building's super, what he'd found. Rodriguez shook his head, made the sign of the cross and told Hector that he'd take care of the situation. Then Hector went outside, nearly slipping on some ice that was left over from the last snowstorm, a week earlier.

When Hector came back to the building a couple of hours later, there was a small crowd in front of the entrance, watching the medical workers remove Mrs. Gonzales's body.

A local TV news reporter stood in front of the crowd holding a microphone and talking into a camera. She said: "The dead woman was Mrs. Maria Gonzales, whom neighbors described as the most caring person they knew. Mrs. Gonzales had a kind word for everyone and was always making meals for the sick, baby-sitting neighborhood children and caring for the elderly. Though she herself was seventy-five and had trouble with her health, she never complained and was much loved here on this Bronx block.

"Everyone knew her, everyone will miss her. Maria Gonzales, frozen to death, in a building that hasn't had heat in over two weeks. Attempts to reach the building's management agency, Atlas Realty, have so far been unsuccessful. Records indicate that Atlas has been cited for building violations over fifty-nine times in the last year, on everything from inadequate heat to rodents to broken pipes. Now, back to you in the studio, Bill."

That night, after the tenants of the building held a meeting to talk about what could be done (they just griped and complained and shook their fists as usual), Hector Nunez went back to his apartment. He sat in the dimly lit room, pulled his fur hat over his ears and sipped some lukewarm soup he had bought at the bodega on the corner. Then he thought about Mrs. Gonzales.

Mrs. Gonzales had been like a mother to him and he would miss her very much. She'd always asked him how he was feeling. Told him about odd jobs that she'd heard about in the neighborhood. Cooked for him. Her rice-and-bean dishes were even better than ones he'd had in a restaurant. He would miss Mrs. Gonzales. But, he decided, life had to go on.

Hector had trouble sleeping that night and dreamt about Mrs. Gonzales. When he woke up, it was still dark. As he lay in his bed, trying to keep his feet warm through the four pairs of socks he was wearing, he decided that he must do something. Something for the memory of Mrs. Gonzales. Hector got out of bed. Since he had slept in his clothes, as he had done for days, all that remained was to put on his shoes.

After he did, he went to the window. Through the metal gates he looked out at the dark, empty streets. Nothing would be done about Mrs. Gonzales, he decided. She would be buried and still there was no heat. And still the ceiling was peeling and the electricity went on and off. How could the people in his building get treated like this, he wondered? Wasn't the landlord a human being, too? No one even knew who the landlord was. The rent was paid to a company in Manhattan. Atlas Realty. Just a name on an envelope. When someone was murdered on the street, the police would look for the killer. Many times they would not find him, though there would be witnesses. Hector was thirty years old and had lived in the neighborhood his whole life. There were more drugs now than there had been when he was a child. There were more killings, too. The law of the neighborhood, the unwritten rule was: you see, but you forget. But Mrs. Gonzales was different. There would be no police investigation, no hunt for a murderer and yet she was dead, just the same as if a gun had shot her. Her death must be investigated, decided Hector, her killer caught and punished. Hector had seen, but this time he would not forget.

A few hours later, Hector took the train into Manhattan. Atlas Realty was located on a quiet east side street, on the third floor of a small building. Hector looked at the building, then walked a few blocks and went into a bar. He spent the rest of the day sitting in a corner of the bar, reading the afternoon paper. There was a small item about Mrs. Gonzales on page fifteen of the *Post*. The article was the size of a postage stamp. It said no more than he already knew.

Hours passed, and night came to the city. At exactly eleven o'clock, Hector broke into the office of Atlas Realty. He looked through file cabinets and Rolodexes, searching for a name. After an hour, he had the one he was looking for. And an address to go with it.

Hector left the small building and went home. The next day he took the subway to Grand Central Terminal.

In the warmth of the railroad terminal he took out his notepad and looked at the name he'd copied down. Albert Smith. Hector put the pad back into his pocket, went over to the ticket booth and bought a round trip ticket to Larchmont.

Hector got out at the Larchmont station and asked a middle-aged woman, who was wearing a fur coat and walking a small dog, directions to the address. She told him. He thanked her, then walked down the tree-lined street. After a while, he no longer was bothered by the wind cutting at his face.

Half an hour later, he stood in front of the address on his pad. It was the kind of house that he'd only seen on TV. Hector stared at the place for a minute and counted the windows. Then he noticed that there was no car parked in the driveway. Hector looked up and down the street. It was quiet. He quickly made his way past the bushes on the front lawn, and into the back yard. In a few minutes he was inside the house.

The place was like a palace, thought Hector, as he examined the beautiful paintings on the walls and felt the plush carpeting on the floor. But, he told himself, he was not there to admire the furnishings. Upstairs he found a book of photographs and then an address book.

Ten minutes later he left the house and walked rapidly down the street.

The Port Authority bus terminal was crowded. Hector went to a ticket counter, bought a one-way ticket to Miami and paid for it with crumpled dollar bills.

Hector slept on the bus. It was the first time in weeks that he had a warm place to sleep. When he woke up, he looked at a photograph that he'd taken from the house he had broken into. The man in the photo was middle-aged, wore glasses, and was smirking.

MANY hours later, Hector stepped off the bus. As soon as he did, he felt the bright sun beat down on him, and he saw palm trees. He had never seen one before except on TV and stared at them for five minutes. Then he found a diner and bought a fish sandwich. Afterwards, feeling refreshed from his long peaceful sleep, he walked around the city.

It was not that much different than New York, Hector decided, except that it was much warmer. On a side street Hector saw kids playing in the water of an open fire hydrant, near a butcher shop. He watched them for a minute, then went into the butcher shop.

"May I help you?" asked the man behind the counter. He had a bloodstained apron.

"I'd like to buy a pound of hamburger," said Hector.

"Of course," said the man, as he pulled out a piece of meat and put it into a grinding machine.

"Pretty hot out there," said Hector.

"Yup," said the butcher, "but when I want to keep cool I just walk into my meat locker."

"Sounds good," said Hector, as he paid for the hamburger.

The butcher gave him his change, then Hector walked out of the store.

Hector gave the bag of hamburger to one of the children playing on the sidewalk. He told the child to give it to his mother.

A few hours later, Hector went to the street listed in the address book he'd found in the house in Larchmont. The street was a quiet one, and overlooked a beach. The house he was looking for turned out to be slightly smaller than the one in Larchmont. There was a palm tree in front of it. And a car. Inside the house were lights.

Hector looked down the deserted street and then went behind the house. He pressed his back against the building and slowly inched his way sideways, till he found a window.

Then, he stole a glance inside. He saw a room with the same kind of paintings that were in the other house and lots of flashy chrome furniture. Just then, someone walked into the room. Hector pulled away. Then, once again, careful not to be seen, he slowly peered inside. He instantly recognized the man. He was the one in the picture. Hector waited a few minutes to see if anyone else entered the room. When no one did, he went to the other windows of the one-level house and looked inside. Five minutes later, he was satisfied that the man was alone. Then Hector picked up a rock, found a door that was unlocked and slipped inside.

Albert Smith was watching television when Hector crept up behind him and hit him over the head with the rock. Smith fell to the floor and didn't move. Hector found Smith's car keys. Then he wrapped Smith in a blanket, carried him outside and placed him on the back seat of the car. A minute later, Hector drove Albert Smith's car out of the driveway and down the street.

Twenty minutes later, Hector parked the car on the side street he'd been to that afternoon. He got out of the car, went to the butcher shop, which was now closed, cut the wires on the alarm system, and opened the door. Then he went back to the car and got Albert Smith.

The next day, Hector took a long walk. It was sunny. People sat on plastic chairs in their yards drinking beer. Children played ball in the streets. Teenagers carried big radios and laughed. Lovers walked hand in hand.

Near the beach, Hector found a small park and sat down on a bench. Two old women were talking. One said to the other, "I don't know what this city is coming to."

"Neither do I. I remember when it was safe to walk the streets. Imagine, they found the guy in a meat locker in a butcher shop."

"Frozen to death," said the other woman, "that's what the radio said. It's ninety degrees and he freezes to death."

"It's a sick world we live in. What kind of animal would do that to someone, I ask you?"

"I don't know, I just don't know."

There was a pause, then one of the women said, "Did they say what the victim did?"

"I think they said he was in real estate or something."

"It's a sick world."

"Very sick." There was another pause. "Did I tell you what Alice did to her hair?"

"No, what?"

"She dyed it blonde."

"No!"

"Yes. If you ask me, it looks terrible, but don't tell her I said so, she thinks it looks great."

Hector stood up and walked to the bus station. It was time to go home. ✗

Tough as Diamonds

by David Waxman

SHE walked into my office that late September morning like a luxury ocean liner plowing into an iceberg, but she wasn't sinking. Her dress was by some designer I could have named if I hadn't been hung over. It was gray and clung to her very nicely. It provided a nice contrast to the ruby pendant hanging around her neck, her auburn hair, and her pale blue eyes. The hair flowed in curls over her shoulders. She looked to be in her twenties and, since she was in my office, probably in some kind of trouble.

"My name's Samantha," she said. "Samantha Henry." The diamond on her left ring finger flashed like a blue flame as she brushed her hair out of her face. "You're drunk and rumpled."

I looked at my suit, a navy pinstripe that had seen better days. It'd been on me since yesterday and yesterday hadn't been one of those better days. I'd slept in my office, in this chair and in this suit, last night.

I put my hand to my collar to straighten my tie. No tie. I saw it on the floor, next to my desk. I reached across the desk for the bottle of Jack Daniel's. It was empty. I put it back on my desk, took a moment to rub my temples, and then looked at Ms. Henry. It was easy to do, looking at Ms. Henry. I could get used to it in a hurry.

"I'm drunk and rumpled, but you can call me Mike. Mike Mason."

"I know who you are, Mr. Mason."

"Okay. You know who I am. What can I do for you, Ms. Henry?"

"I need a private investigator." Her cell phone rang. She reached into her purse, took it out and glanced at it, turned it off, put it back in the purse.

"For?" I asked. The noise from midtown traffic came through my office window and pounded like a jack hammer in my head. I wanted some aspirin.

"I lost my dog."

"Have you tried whistling? He might hear you and come home."

"She, Mr. Mason. Not he. Brandy. An Irish setter." She pulled a photo out of her purse and held it out to me. "Here's a picture." I took it from her. The picture showed Brandy sitting proudly on a well-kept lawn. The dog wore a diamond-studded collar. I couldn't be sure from the photo, but I suspected the diamonds were real.

"She's certainly a fine dog, Ms. Henry."

"Will you find her for me?"

"She must be quite special if you're willing to pay me to find her." I paused and glanced at the photo again, at the collar. Ms. Henry wouldn't be worried about my fee. I continued anyway. "People usually just put up fliers. You know — 'Lost Dog' on top, picture of dog in the middle, 'Reward for Return' under the picture." I tried handing the photo back to her. She didn't take it. I put it down on my desk.

"Please keep it," she said. "Find her for me. She *is* special."

Finding lost dogs wasn't my idea of the best use of my talents as a private investigator. On the other hand, I still owed this month's rent and I'd finished my last bottle of Jack Daniel's. I rubbed my temples again.

"All right," I said. "I'll try to find her."

"Thank you, Mr. Mason." She took a roll of bills from her purse and handed it to me. "Please take your usual fee."

I peeled five one-hundreds off the top and gave the rest back to her. "That's a start," I said. I put the bills on my desk. "Call it my retainer. I'll let you know how much you owe me when the job's done." She nodded and put the remaining bills back in her purse. I picked up the photo. "Where and when was this taken?"

"My parents' place, in Greenwich. June."

"You live with your parents?"

"No. I have a condo in Brooklyn."

"Alone?"

"With my fiancé."

"What does he do?"

"Nothing, really. He lives off my money."

"Your money?"

"My parents' money, my trust fund, if you must know. What does this have to do with finding Brandy?"

"Maybe nothing. Maybe more than it seems right now." I paused, considering what I needed to know to get started. "When did you last see Brandy?"

"Last week, at my parents' house. Jack and I were visiting."

"Jack?"

"My fiancé."

"Okay. You, Jack, and Brandy are visiting your parents."

"Yes. I was in the backyard, with Brandy, and I heard an

argument in the house. Jack and my father, disagreeing about something. I went in to see what the trouble was. It wasn't anything, really. So I went upstairs to powder my nose. When I went back outside, Brandy wasn't there. I tried calling her." She paused. "I even whistled, Mr. Mason. It didn't help. I went back inside and looked for her, but I couldn't find her."

"What were your father and Jack arguing about?"

"Nothing in particular. They always disagree. I don't even remember what it was that time."

"Okay. Your dog's lost in Greenwich. Why would you come to a PI in midtown Manhattan?"

"Don't you want the work, Mr. Mason?"

"Why me, Ms. Henry? Greenwich gotten rid of all its PIs?"

"No, Mr. Mason, Greenwich has private investigators. It's just that my family's rather well known in Greenwich. I don't need or want the publicity — for my parents or for myself. I know I can count on you to be discreet."

I didn't believe her. Private investigators don't stay in business if they sell their clients' stories to the tabloids. I'd be discreet, but so would any licensed PI she might hire. I took a moment to think. Despite my misgivings, I let her explanation ride.

"I don't suppose your parents will be expecting me."

"No." She reached into her purse, pulled out a business card, and handed it to me. The card read, 'Richard Henry, Esq.' and, under the name, 'Attorney at Law.' Under the title were a phone number and an e-mail address.

"Your father?" I asked.

"Yes."

"How can I reach you?"

She reached into her purse again and pulled out another card: 'Samantha Henry' and, underneath, phone number and e-mail.

"Okay. I'll be in touch," I said.

"Please find her, Mr. Mason."

"I'll do my best."

She turned and walked out of my office. I watched her shut the door, then looked at the two cards in my hands. I put them on my desk, then rummaged through a desk drawer, found a bottle of aspirin, took two. I picked up the phone and dialed Greenwich.

A woman answered in a crisp business voice: "Mr. Henry's office. Mary speaking. How may I help you?"

I asked for Mr. Henry.

"May I ask who's calling?"

"Mr. Mason, Mary. Mike Mason."

"From?"

"From midtown Manhattan."

"Oh," said Mary. "Does Mr. Henry know you?"

"Not yet," I said.

"He's in a meeting, Mr. Mason. Can I have him return your call?"

"Certainly." I gave Mary my phone number, thanked her, and hung up. I put my feet up on my desk, leaned back in my chair, closed my eyes, and fell asleep.

Twenty minutes later my phone rang, waking me. I pulled my hand across my face, rubbed my eyes, and answered on the fourth ring. It was Mary.

"Mr. Mason," she said, "Mr. Henry wants to know what your call is in reference to."

"It's in reference to his daughter and her dog."

"Oh," said Mary. She was silent a moment. "Please hold," she said.

"Sure." I rubbed my temples. I opened my desk drawer, found the aspirin bottle, took a couple more.

A moment later, a man's voice, deep, serious, and self-important, said, "Mr. Mason, this is Richard Henry. What can I do for you?"

"Your daughter was in my office this morning. She wants me to find her dog."

"How does this involve me?"

"She told me she last saw her dog at your place."

"Mr. Mason, if my daughter wants to waste her money hiring private investigators to find her dog, that's her business. But I'm afraid I won't be of much help to you. I don't know where the damn dog is and, frankly, I don't care."

"Would you mind if I come out to your place and look around?"

"Yes, Mr. Mason, I would mind."

I was silent.

"May I ask you a question?" he said.

"Sure."

"Where did Sam find you, anyway? I thought she'd been through all the PIs in the tri-state area."

"My office is in midtown, Mr. Henry. I was in my office. That's where she found me."

I thanked him for his time and we said goodbye. I thought a moment, and then dialed Samantha.

"What's your parents' address?" I asked.

She told me. "Did my father agree you could go out there?"

"Not exactly."

"Be careful, Mr. Mason."

I told her I'd be careful, hung up, left my office, locked the door behind me, and went home. Once home, I shaved and put on a fresh suit. I was determined to be clean and rumple-free as I began my dog hunt.

I made the drive to Connecticut in good time and found the Henrys's estate. I drove past, parked my car on a nearby side street, and walked back. Since Mr. Henry hadn't seemed eager for visitors, I avoided the long gravel driveway that led to the three-story brick mansion. Instead, I walked onto the estate through a row of tall pines that paralleled one side of the house. I crossed the lawn, recognizing a wrought-iron bench from the photo Samantha had shown me, and made it to a window. Inside, an Irish setter lay on an area rug in front of a fireplace.

I heard a noise behind me and turned. A fist wearing brass knuckles connected with my left temple. I felt a sharp pain, felt myself falling, then blacked out.

When I came to, I was lying on a couch. A tall man with a shaved head stood over me. His face looked like it'd been the target for a heavy weight in training — and the tall man, as sparring partner, had neglected to wear protective gear. Or, maybe he'd been the heavy weight and taken his share of punishment in the ring. He wore a black t-shirt that barely contained his pecs and biceps, black slacks, and black leather shoes. The brass knuckles, my wallet, and my .38 lay on a walnut side table, across the room. A Tiffany lamp also sat on the table, and a leather armchair was on either side. Two more armchairs, one on either end of the area rug, faced the fireplace. The Irish setter had gotten up off the rug and was standing next to the tall man.

"How you feelin', Mr. Mason?" the man asked.

I put my hand to my left temple and winced.

"Want an ice pack?"

I nodded yes.

He yelled to the house outside the room, "Marsha, bring Mr. Mason an ice pack." He looked down at me. "What're you doin' here, Mr. Mason?"

"Looking for a dog."

"Any particular dog?"

"An Irish setter named Brandy."

The Irish setter standing next to the man put her face closer to mine. I reached up and patted her head. She wagged her tail.

"Think you found her, Mr. Mason."

A woman in a black and white maid's uniform came into the room and handed the tall man an ice pack. "Thanks, Marsha." He handed me the ice pack and I put it against my temple. "Why would you be looking for Brandy?" he asked.

"Her owner told me she was lost and asked me to find her."

"Does she look lost to you, Mr. Mason?"

"You seem to know *my* name. How about telling me yours?"

"Frank."

"Okay, Frank. What are *you* doing here?"

"I don't have to answer your question, but because I'm a good guy, I will. I work here. I make sure the wrong people don't wander onto the Henrys's property."

"Where are Mr. and Mrs. Hen—"

"No," Frank interrupted. "You may be a PI, like your card says, but now *I'm* askin' the questions. Brandy look lost to you?"

"Her owner says she was," I offered. "How about we arrange for Brandy's owner and Mr. and Mrs. Henry to join us, get this thing straightened out?"

"Don't know if that's a good idea, Mr. Mason."

"Look, Frank. I started the day with a hangover. Now I've added a whack on the head. I just want to finish this job and go home."

Frank thought a moment. "Okay, let's see what we can do." He walked out of the room. I held the ice pack to my head with my left hand and reached out to pet Brandy with the other. She wagged her tail. She wasn't wearing a collar.

Frank walked back into the room. "No dice, Mr. Mason. You're going home." I adjusted the ice pack on my head. "You can take that with you, complements of the Henrys."

"I wouldn't want to leave before saying goodbye to Mrs. Henry. That would be rude."

Frank smiled and chuckled. "You're funny. And you're going. Let me help you off that couch."

A woman walked into the room just as Frank was reaching down to help me off the couch. Her face suggested she was in her mid-fifties, but she'd kept a youthful figure. When the face had been youthful, I imagined, she could have been mistaken for Lauren Bacall. She was immaculately dressed in charcoal-gray slacks and a pink silk blouse. Her black hair was put up in a bun and she wore a strand of pink pearls around her neck.

Frank straightened up and backed a step away from the couch. I sat up.

"Ma'am," said Frank.

"Mrs. Henry, I'm Mike Mason."

"I know who you are, Mr. Mason."

"Your daughter knew, too. Must run in the family."

She looked at me impassively, as if she were studying a beetle pinned to specimen board. "What do you want here, Mr. Mason?"

"At the moment, I'd like to understand why your daughter would ask me to find a lost dog that isn't lost."

"Why is my family's business any concern of yours?"

"Why did your daughter hire me to find her dog, Mrs. Henry?"

She turned to Frank. "Mr. Mason can leave now."

"Yes, ma'am," said Frank.

Mrs. Henry left the room. Frank looked at me. "Will you need help leaving, Mr. Mason?"

"No, just show me to the door."

Frank took my wallet and .38 off the table and handed them to me. I put the gun in my shoulder holster and the wallet in my slacks pocket, then handed him the ice pack. "I don't need this. The bump on my head will do fine as a souvenir."

Frank grinned and led me to the door.

As I walked down the driveway, I considered my next move. I'd have to let Samantha Henry know her dog was alive and well at her parents' house. Then I realized I hadn't eaten since dinner yesterday. I made it back to my car, drove into town, and found a diner. It was one of those places built to resemble a railroad dining car — long enough to accommodate the counter and necessary number of booths; only as wide as it had to be.

Inside, the diner smelled of coffee, hot grease, and stale cigarette smoke. An elderly man sat at the counter, a cup of coffee in front of him, reading the paper. A man and woman sat at a booth, food and beverage on the table, eating and talking. I took a booth. Someone had used duct tape to repair a rip in the red plastic seat cover. The table top was white Formica that had yellowed with age. I heard the clatter of dishes and silverware from the kitchen. A waitress came from behind the counter and brought me a menu. 'Mel's Diner,' it said on the front in red stylized script, above a black-and-white photo of the place. 'Serving the Best Burgers Since 1955.' The waitress was a heavyset woman in her forties, wearing the usual waitress uniform. I took Mel's recommendation and ordered a burger with fries and a cup of coffee. Coffee was my second choice. Jack Daniel's wasn't on the menu.

I took out my cell phone, about to call Samantha Henry,

when she and a young man walked into Mel's. She was dressed in jeans, an oversized white t-shirt, and a brown-leather, aviator's jacket. No jewels except the diamond on her left hand. Still easy to look at. He was tall and lanky, with straight blonde hair that just reached his shoulders. He wore jeans, too, with a faded Grateful Dead t-shirt and a jeans jacket. The young man was talking in an animated manner, making some point. Samantha pretended to pout and punched him on his shoulder. He put his hand on his shoulder and pretended to be hurt.

Then she saw me and stopped. She put her hand out and stopped the young man. She said something to him and they both walked over to my booth.

"Mr. Mason," she said, "this is my fiancé, Jack Singleton."

I stood and shook his hand. "Nice to meet you, Mr. Singleton."

He laughed. "Mr. Singleton's my father. I'm Jack."

"Okay. Jack it is. Will the two of you join me?"

"Sure," said Jack. "Thanks, Mr. Mason." We sat. "Sam's been telling me you're gonna find Brandy for her."

"Uh-huh. Only Brandy's not lost."

Jack looked at Samantha.

"What do you mean, Mr. Mason?" she asked.

"Why don't you tell me?" I said.

She took a breath. "I guess you were at my parents' and found Brandy there. From the bump on your head, I'd guess you also met Frank."

"Right both times," I said. "Ever think of becoming a PI?"

She smiled. Jack put his arm around her. She turned the smile on him, then looked back at me and frowned.

"Are you okay?" she asked me. "The bump, I mean."

"Yeah," I said. "Nothing I can't fix later with the right medicine." I made a mental note to myself to find a liquor store on my way home. "Why'd you lie to me, Ms. Henry?"

"Was Brandy all right?" she asked.

"All right?" I asked.

"Was she wearing a collar?"

Jack shifted in his seat but kept his arm around her. The waitress brought two menus to our booth, put them on the table in front of Samantha and Jack. A bus boy brought placemats, silverware, and water.

"Why wouldn't she be?" I asked.

The waitress was back with my order. She put it on the table, then turned to Samantha and Jack. "You two ready to order?"

They ordered. The waitress walked away.

I took a sip of my coffee. "Why wouldn't she be?" I asked again.

"We think Mr. Henry took it," Jack said.

"Why would he take Brandy's collar?"

Jack and Samantha looked at each other. Sam looked down. Then she looked up, at me. "My father doesn't want us to marry, Mr. Mason. He thinks Jack only wants my money."

"Is that what the argument was about the day you lost Brandy?"

"That's what the argument's *always* about," she said.

Jack said, "That day, he — Mr. Henry offered me a check if I'd walk away, never see Sam again."

"For how much?" I asked.

Jack shook his head. "I never saw. I love Sam, Mr. Mason. No amount of money could get me to walk away from her."

I looked at Samantha. I believed him. "So what makes you think your father took the collar?"

"There are real diamonds in it," she said. "It's worth quite a bit."

"The man has more than enough to buy his own diamonds if he wants them. Why would he take yours?"

She shrugged unconvincingly.

"Did you ask for it back? The collar?"

Samantha hesitated, then said, "No."

"Why not?"

The waitress brought Jack's and Samantha's order, set it on our table. "Anything else? More coffee for you, sir?"

"No," I said. "No, thank you." Then, to Samantha, as the waitress walked away, "Why not?"

Jack shifted in his seat again. "Will you help us get it back, Mr. Mason?"

"That depends."

"On what?" Jack asked.

"Ms. Henry, why haven't you asked your father to return the collar? If he has it."

"He has it," Jack said.

"He has it, Mr. Mason," she agreed. "My father wants to write me out of his will if I marry Jack. He doesn't want me to have any money, anything."

I waited.

"Come to my parents' this evening, Mr. Mason. After dinner. Jack and I are going over for dinner. Come over after and talk to my father."

"I don't think I'm one of your parents' favorite guests."

"I'll call them now and arrange it." She took her cell phone from a jacket pocket.

"Wait," I said. "I don't see how this could possibly help you. I don't think your father has the collar and, if he does, I don't see how anything I'd say could persuade him to return it to you."

Samantha dialed. "Hi, Mom." Pause. "Yes, Jack and I will be over for dinner."

Jack took his arm from around Samantha and leaned across the table towards me. "Who do you think took it, Mr. Mason?"

"Mel's," said Samantha, and then, "No, Mother, it's *not* a dive!"

"The butler," I said. "The butler's always the one."

Jack laughed. "They don't have a butler."

"What?" I said. "No butler? Then it must've been you, Jack. Jack Singleton, in the billiard room, with the candlestick."

"Like *Clue*?" he asked with a smile.

"Yes. Whacked the dog and walked off with the collar."

Samantha was still talking with her mother.

"Thank God we know Brandy's alive," Jack said with mock seriousness. "As it is, I'm looking at five to ten for theft of collar. I could've been facing the chair for the murder of an innocent Irish setter."

I smiled. I was beginning to like the boy.

Samantha finished her call. "It's all set," she said. "You should come over at eight-thirty."

"All right," I said. "It's your dime." The waitress brought my check. I picked it up and stood. "I'll see you two this evening." I put a tip on the table, went to the cashier and paid, and walked out of the diner.

I drove up the Henrys's driveway at eight-thirty, parked, went to the door, and rang the doorbell. I heard a dog bark. Marsha and Brandy answered my ring. Brandy wore a plain leather collar with tags that looked new. She wagged her tail. Marsha wore her maid's uniform.

"Good evening, Mr. Mason," Marsha said with a trace of a Spanish accent.

I returned her greeting.

"How is your head, sir?"

"Better, thank you."

"Good." She smiled warmly. "Please follow me."

She led me to some double doors of polished wood and then through the doors, into a large, well-lit room.

"I will let the Henrys know you are here."

I thanked her. She walked out. Brandy stayed. I looked around the room. It was carpeted wall to wall. A couple of upholstered couches and six upholstered armchairs were arranged in two groups, three chairs per couch — all modern, stylish, expensive pieces. A large fireplace was set in one of the walls. Two more armchairs sat facing the fireplace and a coffee table, magazines and an open cigar box on top, sat between them.

I heard voices coming from outside the room and turned towards the doors. Mr. Henry, Mrs. Henry, Samantha, and Jack came through them. Mr. Henry was saying, "But we don't know how it'll play on Wall Street." He didn't seem worried. They were all dressed for the dinner they'd just finished, three-piece suits with handkerchiefs sticking out of jacket pockets and elegant designer dresses. Brandy walked over to greet them. Samantha stroked the dog's head.

Mr. Henry walked over to me and extended his hand. "Good evening, Mr. Mason," he said, neither warmly nor coldly.

"Good evening, sir," I said as we shook.

I put him at about sixty; about five ten and a little heavy. I suspected most of the weight was muscle. He had a full head of gray hair and a round face with thin lips and a pug nose.

"Care for a drink?" he asked.

"Sure," I said. "If you're drinking, too."

"Cognac?"

I nodded. "Thanks."

He went across the room to a wet bar.

Mrs. Henry said, "Welcome back, Mr. Mason."

"Thank you, ma'am."

"I'm sorry we got off to a bad start earlier today. How's your head?"

"How's Frank's hand?" I asked.

She forced a smile.

Mr. Henry called from across the room, "Elizabeth, Samantha, Jack. You'll have one, too?" They all said yes.

"Seems we need your help, Mr. Mason," Mrs. Henry said.

"I'm listening," I said.

Mr. Henry returned with the drinks on a silver tray. We each took one. He put the tray on a side table placed next to one of the couches. "Let's sit," he said, motioning with his Cognac to the couch and chairs. We sat, Mr. Henry, Mrs. Henry, and I on chairs, Jack and Samantha on the couch. Brandy set herself down at Samantha's feet.

"Mr. Mason," Samantha said, "I was wrong. My father doesn't have the collar."

"Who does?" I asked.

Mrs. Henry said, "We think our maid took it."

"Marsha?"

"Yes," said Samantha.

"Have you asked her?"

"No," said Mr. Henry. "We thought you might."

"I might," I said.

Mr. Henry nodded. "Let's finish our drinks first."

I turned to Samantha and Jack. "Have the two of you set a date for your wedding?"

"No, they haven't," said Mr. Henry, firmly.

"Now, Richard," said Mrs. Henry.

"Elizabeth, nothing is decided yet. Nothing."

"Mr. Henry," said Jack, "I love Samantha, not her money."

"Richard," said Mrs. Henry, surprise in her voice, "*what* did you say to them?"

"If they want to marry, damn it, they'll have to make it on their own."

"You are *not* doing that to our daughter!"

"We'll find a way on our own," Jack insisted.

"Jack, there'll be no need for that," said Mrs. Henry. She turned to her husband. "Will there?"

"The boy has no career, no future!" His face was red and his voice tight and loud. He looked Jack in the eye. "The little shit accuses me of taking the collar." He kept his focus on Jack, looking like he wanted to spit in his face. "You've been taking my money ever since you you my met my daughter."

"My money, Father," Samantha said, evenly.

Mr. Henry kept his eyes on Jack. "Where's the collar?"

Jack stood, meeting Mr. Henry's glare with his own.

"Sit down!" Mr. Henry demanded.

"Richard!"

"Stay out of this, Elizabeth."

Mrs. Henry opened her mouth as if to say something, then silently shut it. Her face was drawn. Her hand smoothed her dress over her lap once, then again. Samantha sat silent and still, watching her father and Jack.

Jack took a step towards Mr. Henry. Mr. Henry stood. Out of the corner of my eye I saw Frank enter the room. I glanced at him quickly, keeping Mr. Henry and Jack in my peripheral vision. Frank was in the same black t-shirt and slacks he wore earlier and had added a grey sports jacket. His right hand was at his side. It held a gun. I looked more closely. It was a .45. I moved to the edge of my seat and tried to keep both Frank and the others in view.

Samantha was still watching her father and Jack — who were watching each other. Mrs. Henry noticed Frank, took in a sharp breath, and stiffened. I moved again, slightly, to make sure my jacket was loose. I kept my hands on my knees, where Frank could see them, but made sure I could reach my shoulder holster without trouble.

"Frank," I said, "why don't you ask Marsha to bring us some after dinner mints?"

"She's tied up at the moment."

I wondered if he meant that literally.

Samantha looked at Frank and gasped. "My God, what are you doing?"

"Looking for Brandy's collar."

Now they were all looking at Frank.

"In here?" Samantha asked, surprise in her voice.

Frank nodded. He looked at Jack. "Give Miss Henry the collar, Jackie boy."

Jack turned his glare on Frank. "I don't have it, Frankie."

"I betcha you do."

"Frank," said Mr. Henry, "what the hell are you doing?"

"Trying to get your daughter's diamonds back for her, sir."

"Now, Frank," Mrs. Henry began.

Frank interrupted. "Please stay out of this, ma'am."

She glared at Frank, but was quiet.

Mr. Henry began walking toward Frank. He put his hand out. "Give me the gun."

"Stop right there," Frank said.

Mr. Henry stopped. "You're making a mistake, Frank."

I stood up slowly, keeping my hands where Frank could see them if he wanted to.

Frank glared at me and barked, "Sit down!"

"Your show," I said. I sat, but on the edge of my seat.

"Where're the diamonds, Jackie? Sell them already?"

"Maybe you have them, Frank," Jack said.

"I come in here looking for 'em if I have 'em?"

"Why'd you come in?" I asked.

He looked at me, considering something. "Heard some excitement, somebody talking loud. I come in to see what the trouble is."

"With a gun." I said.

Frank smiled. "With a gun."

"Know where the collar is, Frank?" I asked.

"Yeah."

"Where?"

"Already told you."

"Let me check Jack," I suggested. "See if you're right."

Frank shook his head. "Won't have it on him."

Samantha pushed her hair out of her face. The diamond on her hand caught some light and flashed, as it had in my office that morning. "Frank, you know Jack wouldn't take anything from me." Brandy looked up at her.

"Miss Henry, I'm just doing my job."

"I've had enough of this!" said Mr. Henry. He started across the room, towards Frank.

Mrs. Henry yelled, "Richard!" Samantha yelled, "Dad!" Brandy stood and yelped.

Frank raised his .45 and fired. Mr. Henry grabbed his right shoulder, went to his knees, then sprawled on the carpet. Samantha froze on the couch, her eyes wide. Brandy yelped again but stood her ground in front of Samantha. Mrs. Henry went to her husband and knelt by him. He was breathing hard and grimacing. Jack joined them. He took out his handkerchief and put it on the wound. The white cloth instantly turned red. While Frank was watching them I undid the catch on my holster. I took out my gun and held it at my side, out of Frank's line of vision.

Mrs. Henry reached up for a pillow from one of the chairs and put it under her husband's head. "We have to call an ambulance."

"No," said Frank. "Everybody stay right here."

"For God's sake, Frank! At least let us get a towel to stop the bleeding."

"No, ma'am."

"If you have the collar, Frank," I asked, "why'd you come in here?" I wanted to get his attention.

He looked at me. "Maybe I have it. Maybe I don't."

"If you have it," I said, "you come in here to persuade the Henrys Jack has it?"

He was silent.

"Drop the gun. Let's get Mr. Henry the help he needs."

"I have to think. Shut up."

"Can't do that. A man's hurt. Besides, Frank, I don't like the way you treat me."

"What the hell does that mean?"

"Could've asked me nicely to leave. Whacked me on the head instead."

He hesitated a moment, considering; then his gun began to rise in my direction. Our guns went off together. Frank grabbed his stomach with both hands. Blood seeped between his fingers. He fell. I'd dropped my .38 and now felt pain in my right hand. I took a deep breath, looked down at my hand and saw the wound and the blood. I looked up.

Frank was stretched out on the carpet, reaching for his gun. I could see the circle of blood expanding on his black t-shirt. I moved quickly and kicked the gun away. I wanted to kick him. Jack handed me my .38, then went back to Mr. Henry. I held the gun in my left hand.

Mrs. Henry went to a phone across the room. Samantha joined Jack at her father's side. In a moment we heard the sirens of police and ambulance.

"Jack," I said, "why don't you check Frank's pockets?"

He nodded and went over to Frank. I made sure Frank could see I had my gun. Jack pulled the collar out of an inner pocket in Frank's sports jacket.

Mr. Henry had been watching. "Frank," he growled, "you're fired."

Mr. Henry would live. Frank would live. Next day's paper suggested Frank owed a lot of money to a not so very nice man. It also said Samantha and Jack had set a date for their wedding. I was reading it in the hospital coffee shop.

I finished the paper and my coffee. My hand was bandaged and I'd spoken with the police. On my drive back to the city I thought about the lies we tell each other, thinking they'll keep us together, and the truths, tough as diamonds, that really do. ✗

The Mystery of the Flying Man

by Ron Goulart

HE was standing backstage at the Darkington Empire Theatre talking to his new client when the pack of wild dogs came barking and howling out of the surrounding shadows to attack him. Harry Challenge had only arrived in the Barsetshire town of Darkington late that afternoon. It was the summer of 1900 and he hadn't been anticipating snarling beasts. At least not this early in the case.

Harry was a lean, weathered young man in his early thirties. Folded in the breast pocket of his dark suit was the cablegram that had summoned him from Paris, where he'd just solved a fairly simple case involving the theft of $100,000 worth of black pearls. The message said:

DEAR SON:

OKAY, YOU BEAT THE SÛRETÉ TO THE PUNCH, FOUND THE DAMN JEWELS AND SOLVED A FEW BRUTAL MURDERS. TIME, MY LAD, TO BE UP AND DOING. FORGET FRATERNIZING WITH COQUETTES AND APACHES AND HAUL YOURSELF TO THE DARKINGTON EMPIRE THEATRE IN BARSETSHIRE. ASSISTANT MANAGER, WHO'S FORKED OVER A HANDSOME FEE, WANTS YOU TO FIND HIS MISSING SWEETIE. SHE'S A STRANGE LASS WHO EARNS HER LIVING DRESSED UP AS A MAN AND SINGING DIRTY SONGS.

Just prior to the assault by angry hounds, Harry had been in the shadowy wings of the variety theatre talking over the disappearance of the young performer.

Out on the bright electricity-lit stage a pair of comedy jugglers were tossing items of cutlery at each other while frequently falling over. The large audience, which Harry could hear but not see, was apparently increasingly amused with each new pratfall.

"Go over that again, Foxhall," requested Harry.

Hugh Foxhall, the Assistant Manager of the variety house was a skinny, narrow man of about forty. "I mean to say, Mr. Challenge, that the tradition of an attractive young woman dressing in male attire has long been established in the British theatre, as is that of men donning female garb. That, don't you know, goes back to Shakespeare, if not before. Just the other day a chap was telling me that even the Ancient Greeks went in for —"

"I wasn't referring to Miss Trelawney's putting on a suit of evening clothes, calling herself Burlington Bertie and singing music hall ditties," cut in the detective. "Go over again her behavior just before she went missing."

Out of the bright stage both jugglers fell over at once, yet didn't drop a single knife or meat axe. This elicited the most enthusiastic ovation thus far.

"Emily, the dear sweet thing, when not performing as Burlington Bertie the toff, is a shy and delicate young creature," continued Foxhall. "She seemed uncharacteristically worried and downcast the two or three days prior to her vanishment. Fact of the matter is, don't you know, that she felt so low she was unable to appear at all at the Wednesday matinee. Which disappointed a multitude of her dedicated and enthusiastic admirers who —"

"She didn't tell you why she was upset?"

Foxhall hesitated. "I may have failed to state clearly, Mr. Challenge, that Emily and I are not *officially* engaged," he finally said. "Our romance is, I fear, somewhat lopsided, if you get my drift."

"Another guy?"

"Emily, bless her innocent heart, did have a few other gentlemen friends," the Assistant Manager admitted.

"Was it one of them who was causing her to be upset?"

Frowning, Foxhall answered, "I suspect it was Grant Overman. He's a handsome rascal, well off but no better than he should be. He resides with his father in a dismal mansion in the hills beyond the town. Dear Emily dined with him the evening before she vanished from human ken." He shook his head and made an unhappy sound. "I tried to warn her about Copplestone Manor. Because of the ghost."

"Ghost?"

"For the past few months, several local residents have sworn they saw a dark ghostly figure floating over the Nightwood Forest, which is quite near the Overman estate."

"Have you talked to young Overman and asked him if he knows where she's gotten to?"

"I prefer to have nothing to do with such a bloke. That's why I hired the Challenge International Detective Agency."

Harry asked, "And where does Emily Trelawney live?"

"Emily has been so popular that she's been appearing here at the Empire for over three months. For most of that time she's resided at Mrs. Malley's boarding house on Warner

Lane," said the Assistant Manager. "Her rooms there are quite charming and cozy. So I hear. I mean to say, gentlemen callers are not allowed above the ground floor. Judging by the parlour, where I've spent many a pleasant afternoon listening to dear Emily playing the spinet and singing somewhat gentler songs than she features in her Burlington Bertie turn, the first floor furnishings should be quite nice."

"What does Mrs. Malley say about Emily's whereabouts?"

Foxhall shook his head forlornly. "She's seen neither hide nor hair of Emily since four days ago and has not a notion as to where she might be."

"How about the local constable?"

Foxhall again shook his head. "I have refrained from consulting the law, Mr. Challenge," he answered. "Should it turn out that there's a simple explanation for Emily's disappearance, I am hesitant to set the minions of the law on her trail. Again, that's why I've hired a discreet inquiry agent such as yourself."

Out in front of the electric footlights the juggling duo was taking its final bows, amid considerable applause, hooting, and whistling.

Harry said, "All right, I'll commence by —"

At this point howling, barking, growling, and snarling began off in the shadowy darkness backstage.

"I say," exclaimed Foxhall. "How the devil did Professor Bascom's Dangerous Dobermans get out of their cages?"

There were five large snarling Dobermans in the pack that was moving toward Harry with sharp teeth bared. Deep growls rattled in their black chests as their paws ticked across the boards of the shadowy backstage area.

Very cautiously and slowly Foxhall backed away from the swiftly approaching animals. "Professor Bascom," he called out through cupped, and shaking, hands, "call off the dogs."

Harry, unlike the frightened Assistant Stage Manager, moved closer to the dogs. Squatting, he looked directly at the nearest hound. "Fellows," he began in a calm, steady voice. "I want you all to look directly at my right hand. The one, you'll notice, that is presently drawing lazy circles in the air. Now watch as . . . Hey, stop slithering closer."

The sharp-eared dog just behind the leader suddenly lunged, belly low, and nipped at Harry's dark trousers in the vicinity of his right knee.

"Pay attention, back off." Harry rapped the misbehaving dog on the snout.

Whimpering, it withdrew a couple of feet.

"Watch the moving finger. Fellows, that's right. Keep watching, don't pay attention to anything else. "What's happening is that you guys are growing sleepy, yep. Very sleepy. Good, stretch out on the floor, curl up. Fine."

"I say, this is absolutely amazing, Mr. Challenge."

"Hush," advised Harry. "Stretch out, gang. Close those weary eyes."

In less than a moment more, the entire batch of black-and-tan Dobermans was sprawled and snoring in a slumped half circle around the detective.

Very slowly rising, he quietly asked Foxhall, "Any idea why this Professor Bascom would sic his dogs on me?"

"By Jove, that was absolutely splendid," said Foxhall. "Is that animal magnetism or Mesmerism or just exactly what?"

"A form of hypnotism that my magician friend, the Great Lorenzo, taught me a few years back. It comes in handy now and then," answered the detective as he moved clear of the deeply slumbering dogs. "He picked it up while touring with a Tibetan circus in the 1880s."

"Ah, yes, I've heard of Lorenzo. In fact we —"

"The Great Lorenzo," corrected Harry.

"We tried on several occasions to book his magic show into the Empire," continued Foxhall as he looked down at the hypnotized Dobermans. "Your friend, The Great Lorenzo, however, claims that the management here is made up entirely of cheapskates, misers, penny pinchers, and —"

"What say we dig up Bascom and ask him why his troupe of belligerent canines decided to try to attack me?"

"By George, that is a bit of a facer, isn't it? His act closes the bill . . . " He pulled out his pocket watch. ". . . in just about twenty minutes. Judging by what's just gone on, it's possible Prof, for some reason, may have gone completely bonkers. If not, he ought to be in his dressing room still, applying his makeup. His is the third from the end on the right side of yon corridor." He pointed.

"I'd like to find out his —"

The stage door suddenly came flapping open and a short, thickset man came rushing in, Inverness cape flapping, from out the rainy night alley. "I believe I have the pleasure of addressing Harry Challenge of the Challenge International Detective Agency, do I not?" he inquired as he came trotting across the backstage boards.

"You do indeed. And who might you be?"

"I am Byron Beggarstaff of Her Majesty's Secret Service. I just popped over to warn you, Challenge, that a pack of fearsome hounds is, at any moment going to assault . . . Ah, I now notice I'm a bit late with my warning." He nodded, a bit sheepishly, at the scattered, slumbering Dobermans.

"Just why is British Secret Service interested in me?"

"That should be crystal clear, old chap," said the secret agent as he seated himself atop a sturdy wardrobe truck. "We are, after all, interested in the same case. Once it was learned you were heading here, I was alerted as to a possible attempt on your life. My brother, my twin brother, speaks highly of you. Even though he did the donkey's share of work on that werewolf case at Luddington a few months back, he acknowledges that a few of your suggestions, not the more fanciful ones, you understand, were of help to him."

"In reality, I solved that one." Harry eyed the seated man. "You sure don't look much like Inspector Sexton Beggarstaff of Scotland Yard. You're twins?"

"Yes, I've been asked that question many a time, practically as soon as I was out of the cradle," said this Beggarstaff, sighing. "You see we're not *identical* twins. I wouldn't have minded if I, too, had turned out tall, handsome, whippet-lean, and outrageously popular with the ladies." He sighed again. "But as my dear departed mother explained to me many a year ago, one can't always —"

"How about your getting back to explaining why Her Majesty's Secret Service is interested in finding a missing girl who decks herself out like a toff and sings, 'I'm Burlington Bertie, I rise at ten-thirty?' "

Giving him a perplexed look, Beggarstaff said, "We're not at all, old man. What ever gave you that absurd idea?"

Harry grinned him a thin grin. "Perhaps it was your just now informing me that we were working on the same case."

The secret agent rose from the wardrobe chest. "Do you mean to tell me, Challenge, that you are not in Darkington to gather information as to what Dr Augustus Overman is up to in secluded Copplesstone Manor up in the bleak hills at the edge of town?"

"Nope."

"I say," put in Foxhall, "that old chap is Grant Overman's father, unless I'm much mistaken."

The door of Professor Bascom's dressing room, with considerable creaking, swung slowly open. A short, wire-haired man of about fifty, wearing a stained yellow bathrobe, came tottering out, He noticed his Dobermans scattered in sleep on the backstage boards. "What have you blokes done to me pets?"

"The question I'd like to ask *you*," said Harry, striding toward the staggering dog trainer, "is what your damn mutts were planning to do to me? And who put them up to it?"

THE night rain grew increasingly heavy as Harry walked the few blocks from the Empire Theatre to the inn where he was staying. The recently installed electric lamp posts glowed fuzzily as he made his way along the wet streets.

As he passed a hoarding, the detective suddenly halted to scan a large poster he'd noticed:

See The Internationally Respected Soprano
LILY HOPE
Now Starring in the Delightful Operetta
The Startled Princess
At the Darkington Palace Theatre 10 Days Only!

There was a large black and white photograph of Lily just below the copy. She was a handsome woman in her early forties, a bit on the plump side.

"Talk about coincidences," said Harry to himself as the rain drummed on his bowler hat. "In addition to Her Majesty's Secret Service, we've now got my dear chum, Lily Hope, second-rate singer, first-rate freelance spy." He shook his head. "What in the devil does any of this have to do with the disappearance of Burlington Bertie?"

As he turned away from the rain-washed poster, a female voice behind him cried out, "Harry, hit the deck!"

Recognizing the voice, he dropped to the wet sidewalk.

Up above, from where he'd been standing, there was a loud **thunk**.

Rolling over onto his back as he tugged the .38 revolver out of his shoulder holster, he noticed that a long-bladed stiletto had skewered Lily's poster. Gun in hand, he sat up and scanned the rainy night street. On his right he saw a husky, dark-clad figure running rapidly away. The big man was wearing a soggy black hood. The assailant dashed around a corner, splashing in puddles. No more than a half minute later came the sound of a carriage rattling away into the night.

"Damn, lost the lout." Harry slid the gun back onto its holster.

On his left, standing demurely beside a lamp post and holding a petite, blue umbrella over her auburn-haired head, was a slim young woman. She wore a checkered travel suit. "Only in town a few hours, Harry, and people are already trying to murder you," she said as she approached him. "As I've told you many a time before, you have a real knack for rubbing people the wrong way."

Suit dripping, he arose. "Another damn coincidence," Harry muttered. "Thanks for the warning, Jennie."

"I hate to see someone knock off a friend of mine," she told him, smiling. "What are you doing in town?"

"First, what the hell are you doing? Does it have anything to do with Burlington Bertie?"

The pretty young woman stopped close to him, umbrella held high. "Who's he?"

"She."

"Oh, so?" Puzzled, Jennie shook her head. "No, The *New York Enquirer* sent me over to cover the Floating Ghost story," she informed him. "If you're up to changing into a dry suit, you might take me to dinner, Harry, and we can have a chat."

Putting his hands on her slim shoulders, he grinned. Leaning down, he kissed her on the cheek. "It's the least I can do," he said.

"IT'S not all that strange that we're both staying at the same darn inn, Harry." Jennie was now wearing a fawn-colored, puff-sleeved blouse, a floor-length mauve skirt. There was a white Spanish shawl over her shoulders. "This is one of the few fairly decent ones in Darkington."

"I must admit it has a catchy name," said Harry from across their round dining-room table. "The Golden Violin. Why would anybody christen a place the Golden Violin?"

"You'll find out." Jennie smiled, a slight bit smugly.

"Meaning?"

"I dare not spoil the surprise," she told him. "Now explain to me, in greater detail, why you're hunting for this young lady who calls herself Burlington Bertie."

Resting both elbows on the checkered table-cloth, he replied, "Her plain, everyday name is Emily Trelawney. She's been appearing at the Empire Theatre, from whence she disappeared a few days ago. The young lady apparently earns her living at the moment by donning men's clothes and singing suggestive ditties."

"Sure, male impersonators are quite a fad just now. At least three of them are at the music halls in London the last time I was there. Who's your client, Harry?"

"Her suitor. Well, actually, just one of her suitors. The romance sounds sort of one-sided."

"It sure must be love on his part if the poor simp is willing to pay the outrageous fees the Challenge International Detective Agency charges."

Harry frowned at the pretty reporter. "Hey, my father is the one who sets the fees," he said. "Anyway, this fellow is the Assistant Manager at the Empire. Love is part of it, but he obviously wants Burlington Bertie back to do her act. She's apparently quite a draw."

"What about these wild dogs you say tried to eat you alive?" She took a small sip of her red wine.

"We talked to their trainer, who says he was bopped on the sconce and his dogs borrowed. The fellow who assaulted him wore a mask very much like the guy who tried to knife me," he said. "Professor Bascom, whose act features five mean-minded Dobermans, insists that the masked man must also be a dog trainer, since he got the hounds to go for me. Though it's possible to hypnotize most animals. Which is what I did to avert the attack."

"I bet Lorenzo taught you how to do that."

"He did, yeah."

Nodding, Jennie asked, "And does Lily Hope fit in with any of this business?"

"You knew she was in town."

Jennie smiled again. "I'd have to be a real nitwit not to have noticed those gaudy posters plastered all over town." She said. "She seems to have put on another ten or twenty pounds since last we encountered her."

"I thought she looked quit svelte."

"Since when is svelte a synonym for fat?"

"Does our singing spy tie in with your Floating Ghost?"

"That's quite possible, since I suspect that —" Several of the other diners suddenly groaned in unison. "Oh, good. Here's the surprise I promised you, Harry."

The innkeeper, a jovial heavyset man of about fifty, had entered the dining room. He was carrying a violin and dressed in a Gypsy costume. He strode, chuckling, nodding pleasantly at the various diners, right toward Harry and Jennie's corner table. "Ah, good evening, young lovers." He beamed at them. "You're looking even more petite and sweet than you did last evening, Miss Barr. And your gentleman friend is a fine specimen of —"

"We're merely business associates," she corrected.

"Ah, now I doubt that, miss, I do indeed, judging by the way you look at each other," he countered. "I surely know love in bloom when I witness it or my name isn't Nigel Farquar. Now then, I'll serenade the happy couple with a choice medley of

Romany airs, learned at the knee of my wonderful nanny back in the days —"

"How much?" inquired Harry.

The slightly battered violin halted halfway to Farquar's double chin. "Oh, goodness, sir, there's no charge, not a penny. The violin serenade is absolutely *free* and has become, I must admit, famous across all of England and even some parts of France."

Jennie said, "Harry means how much do we have to pay to have you not play your fiddle?"

The innkeeper was nonplussed. He stared down at Harry. "Can this be true, Mr Challenge, sir?"

Harry gave him a thin grin. "Most evenings, Farquar, nothing would please us more than a violin serenade, even one played on a tatty instrument like that one," he explained, pausing to sip his wine. "However, tonight we happen to be in mourning for a recently departed life-long chum of both of us. He, too, by strange coincidence, was also a violinist. Though his fiddle was in a somewhat better state than that one you're carrying around. We would, therefore, prefer to enjoy our sorrow in silence."

He innkeeper lowered his violin, letting it dangle by his side. "Ah, forgive me, Miss Barr, Mr Challenge," he apologized. "I shan't intrude on you at such a moment. In fact, in memory of your departed friend, I won't play at all this evening. Farewell." Shoulders slumped, he made his way across the inn's dining room and out the door.

Several of the other patrons sighed in relief, others nodded cordially at them, a few applauded quietly.

Voice lowered, Harry said, "You were saying, Jennie?"

"Thank you, Harry dear, for saving us from a fate worse than death," she said to him. "What I was going to tell you, before we were threatened by the violin, was that I don't believe, after spending two days nosing around town and questioning the handful of people who claim to have seen this Floating Ghost, that there's a ghost at all."

"So what is it, then?"

She answered, "Seems to me it's a flying man."

JENNIE, nearly naked, sat up in Harry's four-poster bed and pulled the lace-trimmed sheet up to her shoulders. "Well, what do you think about my theory?"

"Your theory about why we shouldn't become seriously involved?"

She poked her bare elbow into his unclothed side. "No, nit-wit, about this darn case."

"Yeah, it sounds plausible."

"It definitely ties things together."

Leaning on his right elbow, he turned to face the auburn-haired reporter. "Okay, in quite a few situations like this, what the locals think is a ghost turns out not to be. So, sure, this floating ghost could be a flying man. In my own experience, I've never yet encountered a flying man, but . . ."

"From all the descriptions I've collected — from a half dozen people who've actually caught a glimpse of this floating ghost — I'm certain this is really a fellow wearing some sort of portable engine."

"You think this guy has some sort of flying device strapped to his back? Any of your witnesses see anything like that?"

"All of them were scared and took off soon as they spotted this thing come floating over the woods," she answered. "But some of them told me they heard the ghost making a loud sputtering noise as it flew over Nightwood Forest."

"Could be some kind of engine making a sound like that," he admitted,

"Exactly, Harry."

He frowned, glancing up at the purplish canopy over the bed. "Thing is, Jen, inventors have been trying to find ways to fly for quite a while and none of them have quite done it," he said. "In order for there to be a flying man hereabouts, there has to be somebody who —"

"That's where Dr Augustus Overman comes in," Jennie cut in, letting the sheet slip as she pointed at the reclining detective. "He's obviously succeeded."

"Why Dr Overman?"

She pulled the sheet back up. "He's been experimenting for years, trying to develop some kind of portable flying gear," she explained. "I bet he's finally done it."

"Ensconced in Copperstone Manor and not in a big factory or a government laboratory or —"

"He's been tossed out of several manufacturing facilities and at least two British government projects," Jennie said. "He's considerably eccentric. He's quarrelsome, bullying, and his treatment of women leaves something to be desired. He was tossed out of Oxford three years ago because he assaulted a barmaid at a pub called Ye Saracen's Ear."

Sitting up, Harry leaned against the backboard. He was wearing only the lower half of a union suit. "You know quite a bit about the good doctor, Jennie."

"The *New York Inquirer* sent me over to interview him in the autumn of 1897," she said. "He'd just, at his own expense, published a monograph entitled *Icarus Revisited: The Steps Necessary To Creating A Flying Man*. He was experiencing a lot of heckling and catcalls at most of his lectures. That almost always prompted him to leap off the stage and start brawling. A bright, but not a likeable man."

"You figure Dr Overman moved out here, set up a laboratory in Copplestone Manor and . . . what? Finally succeeded in cooking up a flying man and he's been testing his invention some nights out by his place?"

"I do, yes." She gave him a more tender poke in his side. "That would certainly explain why Lily Hope's in town. She's obviously gotten wind of his tests and is going to try to get hold of his secret."

"Yep, that could well be. It also explains what that secret agent I mention, Byron Beggarstaff is nosing about."

"What we have to do next, that is if you don't mind our —"

There was all at once a loud shattering crash. The window next to Jennie's side of the bed exploded inward. Shards of dry old wood and a multitude of clattering, tinkling glass fragments came showering into the dim-lit bedroom. They slammed onto the carpet, bounced on the canopy overhead. Cold night rain invaded the room.

All this was followed by two men who, one by one, climbed in through the dark rectangle where the window had just been. Both wore black hoods. The larger of the two also wore a lopsided black derby. It popped off his head as he landed on the shadowy floor, crunching glass and wood fragments underfoot.

Harry went leaping off his side of the bed, grabbing for his .38 revolver that was resting in its holster on the bedside table.

One of the hooded intruders, the one who'd lost his hat, hopped onto the four-poster, nearly trampling on the startled Jennie, and bounced off, tackling the partially-clad detective.

"No need for violence or firearms, old man," he advised in a cultured, raspy voice as he knocked Harry off his feet and pinned him to the floral pattern carpet. "We're merely here to invite you to a bit of a tête-à-tête."

"I happen to be otherwise occupied just now." Harry managed to bring his knees up into the big man's midsection.

"Ooof," said the hooded intruder as his arms went flapping up.

From up in the vicinity of Jennie's side of the bed came the sound of a bedside lamp smashing against a hooded head.

"'Ere now, mum. Bloodshed, specially my bloodshed, ain't called for no how," said a complaining Cockney voice. "As me mate's been tryin' ter explain, there's really no need fer violence."

Harry, twisting away from his groaning assailant, had tugged his shoulder holster off the table and was easing out his revolver. "You all right, Jennie?" he called out.

"This second lout almost stepped on me."

Harry's hooded lout, taking advantage of this slight distraction, struggled to his feet and, a shade wobbly, managed to kick the holster and gun out of Harry's hand. "As I've been trying to explain, old chap, we —"

Forgetting about his gun, Harry lurched forward and delivered two sharp punches to the hooded man's hidden chin.

"Ooof," he mentioned again, before dropping to the carpet and passing out.

Grabbing him by the collar of his seaman's sweater and his dark trousers, Harry dragged him over to the door of the room. He let go of him, opened the door, gripped him once again, and tossed him into the dim-lit hallway of the inn.

Slamming the heavy door shut, he turned toward Jennie. She now had the sheet pulled up to just under her chin. She was quite alone.

"Where's our other lout?" he inquired as he crossed over to her.

She jerked a petite thumb in the direction of the vanished window. "Took his leave while you were evicting his mate," she answered. "Shouldn't you have saved at least one of them? You know, Harry, to learn who sent them."

He sat down on the edge of the bed. "I'm pretty sure I know who sent them," he said.

WHEN Harry was awakened the next morning by a combination of wagons unloading and donkeys braying in the courtyard below, he noticed that Jennie was no longer present.

Resting on the fluffy pillow where her head should have been was a note. It read, written in the reporter's precise, forceful handwriting:

Harry, Went to my own room to freshen up. Meet me for breakfast downstairs at 8. We can, if that won't upset you too darn much, talk about teaming up on this business. By the way, the innkeeper doesn't play the violin in the morning.
Love, Jennie.

Arising, Harry un-tacked part of the blanket and scrutinized the morning outside. The rain had ended, and a pale watery sunshine prevailed.

He arrived in the inn's dining room at ten minutes after eight.

A half dozen guests were scattered at the tables. Jennie was not among them.

The plump innkeeper, without violin, came hurrying in. "Ah, Mr Challenge," he said, holding a folded sheet of foolscap in his right hand. "I was about to bring this missive up to your room."

"Have you seen Miss Barr?" Harry asked, seating himself at an unoccupied table and accepting the letter.

"No, I regret that I have not. She's a very attractive gel and, to my way of thinking, there's no better way to commence the day than by —"

"Fall silent for a moment," suggested Harry, who'd opened the note.

This one, written in a flowery hand with pale purple ink said:

Harry my dear, Here's what you have to do so that no harm comes to sweet little Jennie Barr. Leave Darkington at once and do not return until Monday morning. She'll be turned loose then. Otherwise . . . well, you can imagine all the terrible fates that might befall her.

Affectionately, Lily Hope. P.S. I am truly sorry you won't be able to attend a performance of The Startled Princess.

Due to the rapidity with which he stood, his chair fell over.

"I say," remarked a gouty old fellow at a nearby table, frowning up from his breakfast kipper.

Harry took hold of the innkeeper's arm. "Who left this letter?"

"Exciting news, is it?"

"Who?" he repeated, tightening his grip

Wincing, the innkeeper shook his head. "I regret that it was left out on the desk whilst I was about my morning ablutions, Mr Challenge," he said. "And what would you like for your breakfast?"

"Not a damn thing," Harry told him. "Where can I hire a horse?"

"Why, right here at our stables, sir. We have three very fine animals for —"

"Saddle one and have it in the courtyard soon as you can."

He let go of the innkeeper and returned to his room to fetch his revolver.

JENNIE, as she regained consciousness, muttered a few words that she rarely used. Then she said, "I know reporting is my chosen profession, but I do wish it didn't involve getting hit on the head so frequently."

"Are you all right, miss?"

Jennie had awakened on a straw mat that was spread out on a stone floor. Kneeling next to her, she now noticed, was a slender young woman clad in white tie and tail coat. "You must be," she concluded as the girl helped her to sit up, "Burlington Bertie."

"Sadly, I must admit that I am indeed," said the young woman. "I've come to feel that this is not the branch of the show business that I wish to follow for much longer. My true name is Emily Trelawney."

"I know." Wobbling some, the reporter stood. The effort made her stomach seem to spin around inside her.

"How do you come to know that?"

"A detective friend of mine has been hired to find you, Emily," she told her as she lowered herself into one of the two wooden chairs the dim-lit, cell-like room contained. "A fellow named Foxhall hired him."

The actress sighed. "Him," she said forlornly. "I don't know how you feel about your detective friend, but I'm afraid I only attract chaps I end up not much caring for."

"Oh, I'm very fond of Harry Challenge."

Emily brightened. "I've heard of him. He's quite famous," she said. "His exploits are often chronicled by an American journalist named Jennie Barr."

"That's me, actually. I'm Jennie Barr."

"I'm certain that a man of Harry Challenge's capabilities will soon find us and get us out of here."

"Quite probably, yes," agreed Jennie. "Now tell me where *here* is."

"We're down below Copplestone Manor. In times past, this was a dungeon and we're locked up in one of the cells."

"And why exactly were you tossed down here?"

Sighing, Emily replied, "Well, the initial cause was another of my unwise infatuations." She sat, uneasily, in the wooden chair opposite the reporter. "Why, I am no longer certain, but for a time I was infatuated with a handsome young gentleman named Grant Overman. He —"

"Augustus Overman is his pappy," cut in Jennie, pointing at the low grey stone ceiling. "He's using this place to work on some kind of flying machine, isn't he?"

"Yes, I found that out, much to my sorrow," replied Emily. "Four nights ago — I think it was four nights, but I've somewhat lost track of time during my stay below ground — Grant sent me a note at the theatre, saying he wouldn't be able to take me to dinner. I had been suspecting that he was involved with another woman. So, not even bothering to change out of my Burlington Bertie costume, I came rushing over to Copplestone Manor. A jealous fool, I intended to confront Grant. I was in the act of crossing the courtyard, when I chanced to look up at the tower. I saw Grant throw himself from the window. Struck with horror, I screamed, quite loudly."

"But he didn't fall," said Jeannie. "Instead he started flying, aimed at the nearby woodlands."

Emily, rubbing at her bowtie, gave Jennie a puzzled look. "However did you know that?"

"Reporter's instinct."

"Grant heard me. He turned back and came flying down to me," continued the actress. "I saw then that he had some kind of engine strapped to his back. I blurted out, 'Why, you're the Floating Ghost!' He, in turn, said, and it's such a theatrical cliché, 'And you know too much.' "

"How come Grant Overman and his dad dumped you in a cell?"

"It's because of the schedule they're on. The senior Overman has arranged to sell his invention to a foreign power," she said. "The agents of this country will arrive in a few days to buy the model and the plans of the invention. These foreigners intend to create an army of flying soldiers."

"So rather than kill you to keep you quiet, they're locking you up until the deal is over?"

"That's it, yes. I assume, since you also seem to know quite a bit about what's going on, that they're keeping you here for the same reason."

"What's to stop us from contacting the Secret Service once we're loose?"

"They don't care. The payment for the secret is substantial. Grant and his wretched father intend to take the money and flee England, settling in some obscure little European country like Ruritania or Graustark."

"We're going to have to make sure they don't get the chance to —"

The oaken door of their cell made a rattling, groaning

noise, then creaked open. "Well, what a pleasant surprise to see you once again, Miss Barr." Lily Hope, a handsome woman in her forties, wearing a floor-length, lowcut, ebony gown, entered the dim cell.

"Myself, I'm not surprised," said Jennie. "Though I thought you'd be trying to steal Overman's invention, rather than working with him."

"If you don't mind, dear, I have something to say to Miss Trelawney," the singer/spy said, a trifle impatiently.

Not replying, Jennie made a slight bow in her direction.

Lily, who was sporting a fairly believable red wig, said, "There's been a change in plans. My clients are arriving tonight instead."

"Does that mean we'll be freed earlier?"

"Most certainly," Lily assured her. "If you coöperate."

"What more must I —"

"We're planning a dinner for our clients," said the spy. "And a little entertainment afterwards, to put them in as receptive a mood as possible. My understudy will appear in my place at the theatre tonight, while I present a medley of Light Opera favourites. My accompanist, who is also a gifted zither player, will render some of the 'Goldberg Variations' as arranged for that instrument." She paused. "To end on a lighter note, you'll do your Burlington Bertie turn. You, I've learned, have quite a following all across Europe."

"I don't feel that I —"

"Oh, but you shall, dear. Otherwise some of my nastier minions will —"

"All right, very well."

"I can do a nifty cakewalk," offered Jennie.

"*You* will stay safely locked down here," promised Lily. "Though I'll have somebody bring you a dish of treacle pudding. If there's any left over."

IT was late in the afternoon when the stone floor of Jennie's cell, which she was now inhabiting alone, commenced rumbling, grinding, grating sounds.

"Yikes," the auburn-haired reporter remarked, jumping up from her chair, as a three foot by three foot section of the floor swung open downward to reveal a dark, earth-smelling black square.

A moment later, Harry, partially festooned with spider webs and crumbs of long-dry leaves, rose up into the narrow room.

After taking a frowning glance at the watch pinned to her checkered jacket, Jennie said, "You sure as heck took your sweet time coming to my rescue, Harry. You weren't swift."

Pushing against the grey floor with both palms, he pushed himself up into the room. He moved away from the trap door opening, brushing grey webs off his trousers. "I was, Jen, unavoidably delayed," he explained. "The town historian had gone fishing, or so he told his wife."

"You felt you needed to bone up on Darkington history before rushing to save me?" She took a few steps in the detective's direction.

"What I actually felt was the need to take a look at the architectural plans of Copplestone Manor."

"Did the historian have them?" She suddenly pointed at his head. "You have a little black spider sitting on your left ear."

Swiping the spider away with the side of his hand, he said, "He well might. But by the time I tracked him to the vine-covered cottage where the off duty barmaid he's seeing on the sly resides, he'd left."

"And so?"

"She proved to be an intelligent, though overly plump, young woman and suggested I see her Uncle Maxwell, the proprietor of the only antiquarian book shop in town," Harry said. "He had a nice set of plans, all tied up with a scarlet ribbon. Showed the dungeon and its hidden entrances. Quite helpful."

"And you figured I'd be here?"

"Seemed like a place that Lily Hope would store you, Jennie."

The young woman left her chair, carefully avoiding the hole in the cell floor. She walked close to him, hugged him. "Figuring out Lily had grabbed me, that's a nice piece of detective work."

"Actually that wasn't too hard," he admitted. "Lily sent me a note telling me she'd snatched you and suggesting strongly that I get out of town for the next few days."

After kissing him on the cheek, she returned to her chair. "I can tell you about that," she said.

Which she did.

HERR Wolfe Knoepflmacher, who headed up the delegation to buy the flying-man invention, shot to his feet from his brocaded chair at the outdoor dining table in the manor courtyard. "Bravo!" he shouted, clapping his beefy hands, the two bejeweled rings flashing brightly in the light from the many surrounding torches. "Encore! Again!"

Dr Overman, who was seated on Knoepflmacher's right, tugged his gold watch out of the pocket of his waistcoat. "It's past time for the demonstration of my invention, Herr Knoepflmacher," he reminded. "My son is even now waiting up in yonder tower, all strapped in to my amazing flying device and —"

"Nonsense! Flapdoodle!" he countered. "Plenty of time, loads of it. But this lovely young lady —" He pointed a fat finger at the nearby temporary stage where Emily, in her Burlington Bertie outfit, and holding the borrowed top hat in her gloved right hand, was taking a bow and smiling, rather uneasily, at the dozen and a half outdoor diners who were politely applauding.

"Encore!" demanded Knoepflmacher in his loud, growly voice. "I absolutely insist!"

Emily looked down questioningly at Lily, who was seated on the customer's other side.

The singer/spy gave a small positive nod, and made a small one-more-song sign.

Nodding, the young woman in the tailcoat and white tie walked across the stage to Lily's pianist, a handsome blonde man of about thirty, and said something to him.

He apparently didn't think much of the song she was going to sing. But he said, "All right, dearie, if you must."

Popping her top hat back on at a jaunty angle, Emily walked up close to the footlights.

"Ever' time I sees me girl

"Hit gets me dander up," she sang in a Cockney accent.

"Marvelous!" shouted Herr Knoepflmacher. "Brilliant! A nightingale for a fact!"

The piano player stopped, gave an exasperated shrug, began playing again.

"An' when I gets me dander up," continued Emily, strutting across the boards.

That idiot!" said Dr Overman all at once.

"Quiet," urged Lily in a whisper," leaning across the ample front of their customer. "It's all right if he —"

The inventor said, "Not him. *Him!*" Half rising from his chair, he pointed upward at the tower that rose up about the brightly lit night courtyard.

Drifting down from the high, wide window of the tower was a dark-clothed man with a stuttering motor strapped to his back and a silvery wing attached to each arm.

"It's that fool Grant, starting the blooming demonstration before that gawky young woman is through with —"

"That's not your balmy son." She was rising up, bending to reach under the flowing skirt of her dark green evening gown. There was a holster strapped to her left leg just above the knee. She started to tug free the .32 pistol nestled in the holster.

Harry Challenge came swooping down. He went sailing over the stage to catch up Emily under her arms. As her top hat fell away, the two of them rose into the air.

The blonde piano player played an angry chord, shut the lid of the piano. "This is deucedly annoying."

Lily, gun now in hand, aimed at, fired at the flying Harry.

The bullet missed but hit one of his wings.

His flight pattern changed, and he and his burden dropped nearer to the cobblestones.

Jennie, who'd been watching from the dark doorway of of a ground-level store room, rushed out onto the courtyard. "Pull up, Harry!"

"Sound advice," he admitted quietly to himself. "However —"

He went smacking into a section of one of the surrounding high stone walls.

His other wing snapped.

Emily, who he found himself letting go of, fell about four feet to the ground and stayed there in an unconscious sprawl.

The strap-on engine was giving off sooty swirls of smoke, loud metallic clucks, erratic ticking.

Managing to stand, Harry was in the process of detaching himself from the damaged engine when the sound of gun shots from several guns sounded nearby.

LIMPING slightly, Harry walked along the early afternoon train platform. Up on the slanting red shingle roof of the station house a half dozen crows sat watching the passengers hurrying to board the waiting train. In his left hand he carried his single small suitcase. Locating his compartment, he set the suitcase down and opened the door.

Jennie was sitting there, eating an apple and reading the latest issue of *The Strand*. Looking up she smiled. "Vanity, vanity."

"I bring you flowers, you give me criticism." From behind his back he produced, with a flourish that rivaled that of his magician friend, a bouquet of a dozen yellow roses.

She took the flowers, set them atop the open picnic basket resting next to her on her seat. "If you hadn't been vain enough to think you could master that flying machine in a few minutes, you wouldn't have crashed and you wouldn't be hobbling around like a —"

"I was shot down," he reminded, sitting opposite her and lifting a small bunch of red grapes out of the wicker basket. "Up until then, I was flying in an exemplary fashion. Fact is, Jen, I noticed several night birds eyeing me with envy."

"Probably vultures, sure you were going to kill yourself."

After eating a few more grapes, he asked, "What did your crass editors on *The New York Enquirer* say about your story?"

"Brilliant, as always," she told him. "Though they suspect I tend to exaggerate your abilities."

"Hard to do."

"And what did your client think of your final report?"

Harry said, "He was, I couldn't help noticing, a bit disappointed. I did find Emily Trelawney, which he was paying us for. And, for good measure, I broke up her romance with Grant Overman. Problem is, she doesn't want to be Burlington Bertie any more and she broke her contract with him."

"From what I saw of her act, I'd say that was wise of her."

Harry finished his grapes. "Myself, I'm sort of disappointed about the way the case ended up," he admitted.

Jennie set the magazine down steepled. "If Beggarstaff of Her Majesty's Secret Service hadn't showed up at Copplestone with a bunch of his men, Lily Hope might have succeeded in shooting you, Harry. Now she's in custody."

"I don't like the idea that he figured out things almost as fast as I did."

"As *we* did. More vanity."

"Hey, keep in mind, that I'm the one who sprang you from that dungeon."

"True."

He grinned. "Can we switch to some new topics?"

"Such as?"

"Well, the question of the state of our romance. For myself, I —"

There was a polite tapping on the corridor-side door of their compartment.

Harry slid the door open. Standing there was Emily Trelawney in a brand new pale blue traveling suit. "I brought you a basket of fruit, Harry." She was carrying a basket twice as large as the one in their compartment.

"Good, I'm collecting them. Are you traveling on this train?"

The actress nodded. "I'm going to catch the boat train. I've signed up for a tour of Europe."

"I thought," said Jennie, "you'd quit being Burlington Bertie."

She sighed "They're very fond of me overseas," she said. "Wolfe has arranged a —"

"That would be Wolfe Knoepflmacher?" asked the reporter.

Emily nodded. "Besides being vitally involved in politics, Wolfe has a great many connections in the entertainment world."

"He's on the train, too?" said Harry.

She said, "Frankly the way I see it, he's an improvement over both Hugh Foxhall and Grant Overman. "

True," agreed Harry.

The actress handed him the basket, kissed him on the cheek and departed.

Jennie smiled across at him, saying nothing.   ✗

A Study in Evil

by Gary Lovisi

THE FIRST DAY

It was after the advent of my marriage, at a time when I lived away from my former room at Baker Street, and my friend, Sherlock Holmes. I had not seen Holmes for months as I was busy in my medical practice. Mary, my wife, was away caring for an elderly aunt, which left me alone for the evening. I was quite prepared to enjoy the pleasures of a tolerable brandy and the latest issue of the *Strand Magazine* when there came a loud knocking to the downstairs door.

"Mrs Hudson?" I was quite astonished to find my old and steadfast landlady from 221 Baker framed in the doorway.

She said not a word.

"What is it?" I asked, concerned as I lead her into the foyer.

"It's Mr Holmes."

"Sherlock?"

"Aye, doctor."

"Is he well?"

She looked at me frightfully sad and nervous. The troubled look on her face told me all I needed to know.

"Give me a moment to get my bag and I will be right with you."

The old lady's hand suddenly grasped my own with a strength I'd never imaged she possessed.

"It's not a medical situation."

"Well then, what is it?"

"Mr Holmes has been arrested."

"Arrested?" I blurted. "Whatever for?"

"It's . . . complicated."

Well, after dashing off a quick note to Mary, I grabbed my coat and followed Mrs Hudson to a waiting cab. The cabby took Mrs Hudson back home, then myself on to Scotland Yard where it appeared Lestrade was expecting me. The dour puss of the police inspector showed his gloom and bad temper. "I knew you would get wind of this, even before the papers did."

"What has happened?" I asked carefully.

"I'm afraid he's done it this time, Doctor Watson," Lestrade said as he led me to a seat in his private office, closing the door behind him. "Sherlock Holmes has gone too far; from solving crimes, to finally committing one."

"Lestrade, that is nonsense." I replied hotly.

"No nonsense this time, doctor. Oh, I am not as slow-witted as you and Mr Holmes make me out to be. I acknowledge that he has bent the rules upon occasion. Upon some occasions bent them quite nicely, and I've looked the other way — for justice's sake."

"But . . . ?"

"But it has gone past all that now. He's being held for murder."

"Murder? That is ridiculous! Sherlock Holmes could no more murder someone than could you or I!"

Lestrade gave me a wry grin that caused me great distress, "Who's to say what any man will do given the circumstances? Regardless, Mr Holmes has admitted to the murder, doctor, or shall I say the assault that has lead to the death of Lord Albert Wilfrey."

"He has admitted it?" I replied, my anger deflated.

"Yes, and quite candidly I can assure you."

I sighed, not knowing at all what to make of such dire news but determined to see my friend at once and get the details of his full story.

"May I see him?"

"Of course, Doctor, I'll take you down to his cell now."

"Holmes!" I shouted, as I ran to the cold iron bars that separated us. I saw that my friend was seated on the jail mattress, as calm as could be, reading a book.

"Watson, I knew you would come."

"What has happened? Why are you here? Surely there is some miscarriage of justice. A mistake?" I rambled, while Lestrade unlocked the door to Holmes's cell, and Lestrade and I entered.

"I'm afraid, it is as Lestrade has no doubt told you," Holmes said in his usual cold analytical manner but there was a softness around his eyes and the slightest tremble upon his lips to let me know he was indeed touched by my presence and concern.

"Please," I stammered. "I am in need of some explanation."

Holmes smiled, "Of course, good Watson, and you shall have it, just as I gave it to the inspector here."

"He admitted it all, Doctor," Lestrade chimed in eagerly.

"Indeed I did, and why not. It is quite cut and dry. I was called out to the home of Lord Albert Wilfrey upon a question of inquiry. You will remember, Watson, that Lord Wilfrey is a peer of the realm and quite influential, a man of great wealth and power. When such a man calls for assistance or council, it is advised you heed that call."

"He is dead?" I asked nervously.

"Oh, most definitely dead, I can assure you, Watson; but please, you are getting ahead of things. Let me explain."

"I feel I need to warn you, Mr Holmes, anything you say here can be used against you at the assizes," Lestrade stated.

"Of course, Inspector, and I appreciate your reminding me of the fact, but what I say now will be nothing more nor less than what I have told you in your official interrogation of me when I called you to the Wilfrey home."

"Then go on, Mr Holmes," Lestrade said.

"It is rather simple and straightforward. Lord Wilfrey and I had a disagreement that escalated quite quickly. Things were said, the situation spiraled out of control, and in my anger and rage I struck him. He went down, hitting his head upon the mantle of the fireplace as he fell back. When I examined his prone form I discovered that he was dead. I immediately sent out one of the servants to fetch the Inspector."

"Upon examination of the body, Doctor, we found Lord Wilfrey had a head wound that corresponds with Holmes's story, and there were some drops of blood on the fireplace mantle where his head struck," Lestrade explained.

I was astonished. Holmes a murderer?

"Surely it was self defense? He struck you first?"

"No, Watson, I landed the first and only blow."

"Then surely it was some kind of accident? You did not intend to kill him, I am sure."

"No," Holmes admitted slowly, "but the result speaks for itself."

"That's all for a judge and jury to decide, Doctor; but for now it's a murder case all right, murder pure and simple," Lestrade interjected.

"Poppycock!" I bellowed.

Holmes smiled, "Oh, Watson, you *are* a true blue friend."

"And you are no murderer!"

Holmes remained silent.

"Well, what of any witnesses? Did the servants see anything that could help your case?" I asked hopefully.

"Lord Wilfrey and I were quite alone when the incident took place," Holmes said softly.

Suddenly I was at a loss for words, aware of a gnawing void deep in the pit of my stomach.

"Of course, we will give Mr Holmes every comfort here, until the trial, Doctor," Lestrade offered.

"Until the trial. Are we not to expect he will be released until the date of that trial?" I asked the inspector.

"Afraid not," Lestrade said sternly. "It is a murder case, after all. Lord Wilfrey was a man of considerable influence and power. Once the press gets word of this . . . well, you know how the papers are with sensationalism? The Yard can hardly allow a murderer . . . I mean a man accused of such a murder to be let lose, you understand. When I took Holmes back to his rooms to collect some personal items and books, no doubt that is how his landlady discovered the situation and alerted you."

I shook my head in frustration and looked at Holmes who only shrugged as if the entire affair was a mere inconvenience rather than the possible end of his brilliant career, and perhaps his freedom and very life.

"Holmes, what of your solicitor? Why is he not here?" I asked.

"I have not called one," Holmes said simply.

I was aghast and said so, "Then I shall get you one immediately."

"No, Watson."

"No?" I said sharply.

"No, I shall conduct my own defense. I am fully capable. In the meantime I shall also get some valuable reading done."

"Reading? And you have not employed a defense attorney? You are on charge for murder, your very life is in the balance! I say, Holmes, you seem to have a damn cavalier attitude toward this abominable injustice!"

"Good old Watson! I see you are fired as usual with that righteous emotional fuel you seem to possess in abundance." Holmes said with a smile. Then he yawned expansively, "And now, gentlemen, I'm afraid you must take your leave."

"Well, I don't believe this entire situation for one minute!" I barked.

Holmes smiled, "I knew you wouldn't, John, and thank you."

I looked at my friend carefully then, trying to gauge any sign from him that perhaps his words held some deeper meaning but his face was as stoic and inscrutable as ever when he did not want to give the game away.

"Something is most certainly up with this," I said boldly.

Holmes only shook his head; "It is what it is. Come see me tomorrow, Watson."

Then Sherlock Holmes turned away and sat down upon his bunk. I watched as he picked up one of the many books Lestrade had allowed to be brought into his cell and he began reading. I was rather surprised to see the title of the book was *Crime and Punishment* by the famous Russian novelist, Fyodor Dostoevsky.

THAT NIGHT AND THE NEXT DAY

I can say with all candour that I slept little if at all that terrible night. Even with my wife, Mary, still away, and me alone, the quiet of our flat grew to be desolate and alarming. It was as if the very walls were closing in upon me — as they most certainly were closing in upon my friend, Sherlock Holmes. How had this travesty happened? I could not wait until the morrow when I would see Holmes again for explanation. My mind was awhirl with all manner of fancy theories and conjectures. Why had Holmes admitted the crime? Why had he not engaged a legal agent for his defense? There was more to this than met the eye, I was sure; and yet it seemed to be cut and dry, just as Holmes had stated; and that had me very worried.

And yet, the more I thought about it, Lestrade's words kept hammering at the back of my mind — of how Holmes had so often bent the rules in his cases — sometimes with even myself believing he had gone far in excess. Could it be possible? Could Sherlock Holmes *be* a murderer? Did the argument and the rage he felt at Wilfrey cause him to strike out with such dire consequences? It seemed so unlike my friend, and yet . . . And yet . . . was he not even now reading Dostoevsky's dark tale in his jail cell — a tale that I knew held as the central character a man who takes it upon himself to kill a vile and unscrupulous monster — thus ridding the world of an evil parasite. The book is about a man who believes murder is permissible in pursuit of a higher purpose. Had Holmes descended into some similar errant vigilantism? I was fearful such doubts could take sway over me.

I shook the cobwebs from my mind as the first glimmer of dawn and a new day approached. I washed, shaved, dressed, and was determined to make some inquiries on my own that morning, well before I visited Holmes that afternoon.

I took a cab to the Wilfrey estate. It was an imposing pile with large, gated grounds. I was allowed entrance by James, the butler, an old family retainer. We had a good discussion about the events of that dark day. He admitted nothing but I could see quite plainly he was hiding something, so I pressed him hard.

"Did Lord Wilfrey leave a widow?" I asked.

"No sir, she passed away years ago, in child birth, sad to say."

"So there are no children?"

"Yes, one, a boy. Young master Ronald is upstairs in his room, indisposed. You can not see him."

"James, please, I need your help." I pleaded.

"You say you are Mr Holmes's friend?" James whispered finally.

"Most certainly," I assured him.

"Then drop this inquiry, Doctor. It is what Mr Holmes would want you to do."

Well, there it was, certainly something nefarious was going on here and now. I was more determined than ever to get to the bottom of it.

"I'll not drop it! Sherlock Holmes faces trail and the assizes for murder — a murder I am now sure he did not commit. Conviction will destroy his career and may end his life! You will have his blood on your hands — and my most fearsome revenge, I can assure you — if you do not come clean with all you know."

James resolve buckled at my threats. Suddenly he broke and told me the entire story. Later he brought in two of the servants, Gloria the chambermaid and Ricardo the groom, both of whom had also borne witness to the incident. I was astonished by what I learned. Holmes had three excellent witnesses and yet he had pledged them all to silence.

Later that day I visited Holmes in his cell at Scotland Yard. Once Lestrade left us and we were alone, I put what I had learned to my friend as plainly as I could.

"I've been to the Wilfrey home, I've spoken to James, Gloria, and Ricardo. You have three witnesses to verify your innocence. Tell me now, what is this all about?"

"Watson, you have become a veritable bundle of energy and ingenuity as you have grown older."

"I have learned from the best."

Holmes smiled then. "So you have cracked James, made him talk? I am sure it took some time."

"I had nothing but time."

Holmes nodded, "And you never doubted me, not for an instant?"

"Dostoevsky? Really, Holmes, that was a nice touch and almost had me considering the unthinkable, but that's just it, isn't it? It is unthinkable — you, a murderer — never!"

"Bravo, Watson!"

"So who are you covering for? Your witnesses would not admit all the details. When do you intend to end this abominable charade?"

"Soon, old friend. I need to give him another day to get out of the country before the pursuit grows hot on his heels. Then I can allow the Wilfrey servants to come forward and tell their tale to clear me."

"But why, Holmes? Why keep me in the dark?"

"Long-suffering, Watson, I am sorry. I never intended this to get so far afield and out of hand. Good Mrs Hudson grew alarmed when Lestrade brought me in cuffs to my rooms to collect some personal effects and books, to make my stay here at least bearable. Since you have moved out into your own flat with wife, Mary, I did not want to alarm you unnecessarily with my plan. Mrs Hudson contacted you before I could give you any of the details. I will give you those details now."

SHERLOCK'S STORY

"I did indeed go to the Wilfrey residence on that dark morning. Lord Wilfrey had arranged to employ me upon a niggling matter of some missing jewelry belonging to his deceased wife supposedly taken by the kitchen porter, Morrow. Well, I brought the man in for questioning, and after that I called for Lord Wilfrey's son, Ronald. That cleared up the matter easily enough. You see, the son had hidden the items, and he readily admitted it when Morrow was accused. It seems the boy and Morrow had become close friends in his short time of employment in the home. The boy is certainly a troubled lad, but he did not want to get his friend fired or arrested for the theft."

I nodded, listening intently, absorbing the facts of the story.

Holmes continued, "However, while I was in the Wilfrey home I am sorry to say that I bore witness to such horrendous brutality that I can only call it by its true name. Evil."

"What was it, Holmes?"

"You know my feelings about the dark secrets that go on in all those pretty country houses, Watson? How I have said quite often that I believe the lowest and vilest alleys in London do not present a more dreadful record of sin than does the smiling and beautiful countryside."

I nodded.

"Think of the deeds of hellish cruelty, the hidden wickedness which may go on, year in, year out, in such places, and none the wiser," Holmes added.

"Yes, you have spoken upon it at times, quite detailed I remember, during the case I chronicled a few years ago in the *Strand* as 'The Adventure of the Copper Beeches.'"

"Well, keep those thoughts in mind as I tell you that no sooner was the kitchen porter, Morrow, brought into the library to confront Wilfrey and myself about the theft, I recognized him as John Maulin Morrow, a young roustabout and violent felon."

"Now I see, Holmes!" I blurted, aware of a criminal connection.

"Not quite, good fellow, and certainly not the entire story. Allow me to explain. I recognized Morrow forthwith, and he me. You see, we have a history. He is a brute and a violent fellow, and yet not all that he seems. I know something of the man, his family life. To be fair, as a youth he was the victim of a vicious homicidal mother. The woman murdered her husband, got away with it, then she systematically tortured the boy. He was eventually taken away from her and put into an orphanage. She died soon after, and the boy descended into brutality and crime."

"Holmes continued, "Young Morrow assaulted a man. Morrow saw him beating a woman. The man was a pimp and the woman a lady of the evening in his employ. But it made no difference, the assault was violent and bloody, it cried out for a remedy. Prison for Morrow was the result. I watched his career over the years, noted his struggle and his progress. Morrow reformed during his time in prison, so much so, that the warden himself gave him a recommendation and he was able to find an honest job. There he met Lord Wilfrey, who offered him the position of kitchen porter in his home. A decision that ended up costing Wilfrey his life."

"The brute! And after Wilfrey had shown him such kindness and taken him into his own home."

"Hah! Not quite, Watson. You see, Wilfrey's son and Morrow struck up an immediate friendship — it seems Morrow saw in the boy something of himself at that young age — and more so, he easily noticed the abuse. . . ."

"Abuse, you say?"

"Beatings of the most violent sort, done to the boy by his own father. It seems the wife died in childbirth but the child lived — Ronald — the father forever blamed the son for the death of his wife. He took it out on the boy with terrible results. I tell you, John, as a medical man, were you to examine this child you would discover the marks of horrendous acts perpetrated upon his person. I believe the boy has, at one time of another, had almost every bone in his body broken by this abuse. The beatings were so severe, young Ronald should have died a dozen times. Such is the power of his steadfast character and heroic will to survive that he has lived this long. It is pure evil, Watson. What has been done to this boy by his own father is nothing less than evil."

Holmes was quiet for a moment. I sighed and digested these facts solemnly. As a medical man I was well ware of such atrocities and had sadly seen my share of them when distraught mothers brought children with "accidents" into St. Barts. Accidents that were clearly the results of beatings, or worse.

Holmes continued, "Of course I had made up my mind to report the matter to the authorities when the situation was suddenly wrenched out of my hands forever."

"My God, was it Morrow?"

"Once I confronted the boy and he admitted the theft, Wilfrey flew into a diabolical rage and attacked the child like a madman. The brute grabbed his son and began to pummel him with his fists. It was tragic, shocking, and so sudden and unexpected. Wilfrey is a big man, six feet in height and over 200 pounds; the boy is but two stone soaking wet. This was not normal parental anger, nor the justifiable punishment of an errant child, it was excessive brutality of the most violent form. I truly feared for the boy's life. So did John Morrow. As he was nearer to Wilfrey than I, he reached the man first. Morrow let go with a massive fist to Wilfrey's chin that hit him with such power it caused the peer to release his hold upon his son and fall backwards. That is when his head hit the lintel of the fireplace. Wilfrey was dead immediately and my examination of the body confirmed it."

I looked at Holmes closely and saw the tragedy played in his features.

"What happened next?" I asked

"Well, of course the ruckus attracted the entire staff. James the butler, Gloria the maid, even Ricardo the groom were all witnesses to the event."

"What a tragic story. And the boy? How is he?"

"Badly done up, I'm afraid. I had the staff whisk him away, after I made them promise not to utter one word to the police."

"So you took the blame. But why?"

"To keep the boy out of it, allow him some solace, but also to give John Morrow the time he needed to escape the country. He deserved that much, I believe. You see, he had truly reformed his life, lived honourably for many years, but after what he and I were forced to witness that day I can not blame him for the action he took. As God is my judge, Watson, were I to have reached Wilfrey before Morrow, I would surely have preformed the exact same action — probably with the exact same results."

There wasn't much I could say after that. I looked at Sherlock Holmes, at the cold iron bars of his jail cell. "So what do we do now?"

"You do nothing. Say nothing of what you have learned. Tomorrow morning, as planned, James the butler will visit Scotland Yard and lay it all before Inspector Lestrade. He will tell what he and the staff witnessed, and then the search will begin in earnest for John Morrow — who will by then be well out of the country, perhaps in America or Australia or God alone knows where. And I wish him well."

"Shall I come back for you tomorrow morning then?"

"Will you? I would be most pleased to see you when this affair is over and done with," Holmes said with a smile. "But mind you, not too early. John. I want to sleep late, as I plan to finish reading *Crime and Punishment* this evening."

THE DAY AFTER

Lestrade led me down into the basement where the jail cells were located and we found Holmes already up and dressed waiting for us.

"Sherlock Holmes," Lestrade said testily, disappointment written upon his face. "There has come forward some witnesses with new evidence to clear you of all charges. You are to be set free."

"Thank you, Inspector," Holmes said, ready to leave, his copy of Dostoevsky's classic novel under his arm. "And good morning to you, Watson."

"Good morning, Holmes." I said softly.

"Yes, good morning all around, I'm sure," Lestrade said stiffly. Something was eating at his craw and he was in earnest to speak up. "I am releasing you, Mr Holmes, but once again you have interfered in official police work. Your admitting to this crime covered up Morrow's killing and allowed him the time he needed to escape. I am not sure we will ever bring him to ground now."

Holmes nodded, "I can not say I am sorry, Lestrade. I know you are angry with me and you may rightly want to prosecute me for my interference . . ."

Lestrade softened and gently placed his hand upon the shoulder of Sherlock Holmes. It was an almost loving gesture, so much so that I was taken aback and barely knew what to make of it.

"I have seen the boy, Mr Holmes," Lestrade said simply. Did I see a tear welling in the tough policeman's eye? "I imagine sometimes, a crime may be acceptable in order to defeat a greater evil."

My companion nodded. Nothing else need be said.

"Well, now Watson, let us leave this place. Will you accompany me back to 221 B, and perhaps we will have a well-deserved luncheon together?"

"Absolutely, Holmes."

"Then good day to you, Lestrade," Holmes piped on his way out.

"And to you, Mr Sherlock Holmes . . ." Lestrade laughed now, *"until the next time."*   ✗

THE BALLAD OF THE *GLORIA SCOTT*

by Len Moffatt

Have you heard the story of the *Gloria Scott?*
She wasn't a schooner and she wasn't a yacht.
As a matter of fact she was a bark —
Not to be confused with a barge or an ark,
And her passengers were prisoners — a criminal lot,
Being transported on the *Gloria Scott!*

Now Sherlock claims that the *Gloria Scott* mystery
Was the very first case in his crime-solving history.
As a matter of fact all he solved was a code
And did some minor deducing at his host's abode.
The victim's memoirs revealed the actual plot
Of the prisoners transported on the *Gloria Scott.*

The prisoners revolted and massacred the crew!
The prisoners were killers except for one or two.
They were put off on a boat with a few supplies —
Then the *Gloria Scott* exploded before their very eyes!
They looked in vain but the ship was gone from sight —
She was obviously the bark that did nothing in the night . . .   ✗

Max's Cap

by Jean Paiva

MAX was dying. What amazed me was that it was here, in a hospital, and not on the street. Max should have died in a pool of blood, shot full of holes. Or, maybe, with his throat cut from ear to ear, his mangled voice box never to growl another demand. Standing there at the foot of his bed, I even told him so.

"Hey Max, what'cha doing lying here, taking up good bed space for. You're supposed to be out there, driving off into the sunset. You know, like a cowboy, with your boots on."

Of course, the moment the words were out of my mouth — make that my motor-mouth and no amount of knuckle rapping from Max over the years had slowed the flow of words from my lips — my stomach turned into a rock with my guts knotted around it for good measure. Grimacing, I stood waiting for the usual fury my loose lips unleashed.

"One thing, Charley, you'll never change," rang Max's still booming voice, followed by his usual gruff laughter. My thinking that Max didn't sound all that sick or dying quickly changed when a wracking cough broke up his words. Gasping for breath, Max still had to have the last say.

"But you always had a knack for hitting the nail on the head, my friend," he said in a more subdued voice, trying not to set off another coughing spell. "This time I've got to agree with you a hundred percent. I should be driving my new Caddy down the expressway, looking at the harbor with a beautiful blonde by my side — remember Mitzie, she was a pistol — and, well . . ." Max's voice trailed off. "That's what you had in mind, huh, old pal?"

"Well, Max," I started, hesitant to share my blood-soaked vision, "sort of." Actually biting my tongue to keep the truth from blurting out, I wanted — for once — to keep my trap closed. This one time I was going to remember Max's constant criticism: "For Pete's sake," he'd yell, "just think for one second before you open your trap and give away the family's secrets! Your motor-mouth goes faster than a supersonic jet. And you wonder why you're always the last one we tell anything."

That was sort of an exaggeration. I mean, I never gave away any secrets or anything. Not once. Well, I don't think so, anyway.

Max probably wasn't remembering the time my motor-mouth got us out of a real jam with Sugar Joe. Joe was ready to pull the trigger the minute he saw Max but I was there and somehow I managed to talk circles around the old guy.

Joe'd had it in for Max for a long time but when Max got the okay to move a fresh load of television sets — you know, the kind that usually fall off a truck — Joe finally slipped a few gears. He wanted to take Max out, then and there; and he had a heavy .45 handy to accomplish this goal. Joe's eyes were glazed and he was looking for a clear shot when somehow I managed to catch his attention. I kept Joe going for a few minutes, talking about the Met game of all things, just long enough for Max to get the gun away.

Sugar Joe gave up after that. Guess he figured he'd had it. Not only was he losing bids to Max, he was even getting sidetracked by some dumb old motor-mouth.

After that we got more and more contracts. As many as we could handle. We probably could have gotten all of them but Max wanted to keep our operation small — and safe. Furs had been big for us for a few years, especially with Sugar Joe out of the way; and Max always said it was my doing. I guess that's why he put up with me. He called me his good-luck piece and told people that he'd rather have Charley along than any rabbit's foot.

Max's brittle cough brought me back to the hospital room, now deep in shadows. Max always liked the dark and other than when he was showing merchandise by bright light — he'd always taken pride in the quality of his goods — only the dimmest lights were on in his home or in his corner of the club room.

"Charley, listen to me." Max sounded very tired. "You're the only one I wanted here, you know I wouldn't even let those other mugs visit. I want to be sure you take care of things for me. Even with your big mouth, you're the only one I trust."

I heard somewhere that praise from Caesar — some Greek god or something in case you don't know — was praise indeed. That's the way I felt right at that moment. Like some god had told me I was the best, which I thought Max was, and he did.

Seeing that my mind was wandering, Max was always good at that, he uttered his favorite curse at me. Not because it's unprintable, which it sort of is, but more because it's personal and private, I'm not going to repeat it but, as usual, it got my full attention.

"Listen up. You're going to take care of some stuff for me." Max went on and detailed a long list of errands and chores I had to do and, even with my mind fully occupied taking notes on the back of his hospital chart, I realized he was dictating his last will and testament.

Most of what he rattled off had to do with what to do with which stuff. There was sure lots of stuff and lots of things to do. Some of it he couldn't seem to decide about and told me to do what I wanted. Later, when I thought about it, I realized he was giving the stuff to me. But back in the hospital room I was just writing down his orders.

When he was through he looked a lot more peaceful. Like he'd gotten a burden off his chest. His ex-wife and daughter were taken care of, as always, and his current girl-friend, Shirley, better be happy with what he was leaving her. Diamonds ain't to be sneezed at. Fortunately for her, Shirley was the last in a long line of leggy blondes. Max could go through dames faster than I could use a box of Mr. Coffee filters.

His new Caddy was the only thing that had his real name on it and, even though he knew I had my eye on it, his daughter was going to get it to replace her station wagon. I knew I could work out a deal with her. She'd never use the long sleek sedan, not with all the kids she had to squire about.

Visiting hours were just about over. The floor nurse poked her skinny nose in the room and arrogantly told me to leave. She had an attitude ever since Max won the battle to keep the lights off. Nurses don't like losing arguments.

"Listen kid, you better take a day or two off from visiting," Max said just as I was reaching for the door. "I ain't feeling so hot. But do me one more favor. My cap, right here on the night table, needs a cleaning. Bring it in for me, will you, so it'll be like new when I get out. And I'll talk to you later."

I realized, even then, that Max didn't quite mean what he was saying. He meant something else but it wasn't the best time to ask him what he really meant. So I took the cap and closed his door gently behind me, not really thinking that I wasn't going to be seeing Max any more.

THE cap was a snap-brimmed tweed, mostly brown and white but with lots of flecks of other colors. A little blue, a little red, even a little yellow. I'd always liked it and had even bought the same cap for myself but when Max saw it he snatched it off my head. "What do you wanta do?" he'd said, "Look like twins?" My cap ended up back in the store.

Leaving the hospital I twirled Max's cap in my hand, liking the feel of it. Without really thinking, I flipped the cap on to my head. It wasn't until I'd started up my Ford LTD and looked in the rear view mirror that I realized I was wearing Max Babson's cap.

It was made for me. The bits of blue picked up the exact color of my eyes, and the brown and white flecks perfectly matched my graying brown hair. All of a sudden I understood what my wife meant when she talked about a dress that she had to have. The cap was me.

It was too early to go home so I headed for the club. Don't get me wrong now, I'm not talking about a country club or a health club or any of those weirdo places. This was the club. The one where Max had his own table. Our club wasn't one of those dinky storefronts, either — where you could look in through dusty windows and see guys sitting around doing nothing. Our club was a double-wide storefront with heavily curtained windows so no one could look in. A small bar had been set up in back and we went by the honor system, leaving cash or chits in the kitty for anything we took.

PULLING up, I found a parking space waiting for me right in front of the club — something I could only remember happening maybe twice before, and the last time was a good five years ago. Checking the LTD's rear-view mirror to see how much space I'd left the guy behind me, I noticed the cap again. It felt so good, like it was meant for my head, I'd forgotten I was wearing it. Flicking the cap's brim with my fingertips I made a quick decision to leave it on. After all, Max had given it to me.

The guys in the club all asked about Max and I told them. He wasn't good. Hank was the first to notice I was wearing Max's cap. It was then, I think, that the guys really believed me about Max maybe not making it.

I took my usual seat at Max's table, on the left side, with my back against the wall. The table itself was to the right of the bar and one of only two large tables in the club room. The other large table was to the left of the bar and it usually held Hank and his crew of dead-beats. There were four smaller tables between these two and the front door, plus a long table under the front window running almost the width of the club, from the wall to the door. On a busy night a couple dozen guys could be found with poker hands and poker faces, brewing it up.

Looking at Max's corner seat I realized that he probably would never sit there again and I got a little misty. It suddenly hit me that someone else might sit in Max's chair and for some reason that was the last thing in the world I wanted to happen.

So I shifted over to Max's chair. At least, I reasoned, it would keep some one else from sitting there.

A couple of beers, a few quick hands of poker and I knew it was long past the time for me to go home. At the request of us members the club had no phone so, if I was to call the wife with excuses, I had to do it from the street. Figuring excuses weren't necessary, that I'd show up soon enough, I got my jacket from the back of the chair and started out the door.

"Hey Charley," Hank called from the bar, "you tell Max we're thinking of him. Especially who's going to get the next contract. There's a load of video tape recorders that's up for grabs." Hank's laugh hurt me. I knew Hank would cut his own mother out of a bidding, but it just struck me as wrong that he was so enthusiastic about the business.

STARTING the LTD up and moving out to the corner light kept me occupied for the next few minutes, but waiting for the green signal gave me time to think. If Hank is ready to move in, the other guys probably also are — but at least they're cool enough not to show it. The green light blinked on and I moved out, still thinking. "What would Max want me to do?" Motor-mouths like me talk to themselves a lot, or so I've been told. Sometimes we ask questions out loud, even when we think there's no one around to answer.

"Bid, you idiot," rang Max's growl, as clear as if he'd been sitting next to me.

Not counting the car I crashed into, I think I handled the situation pretty well.

Pulling over four blocks and two turns later, I sat quietly — very quietly — waiting for the shaking to stop.

"Bid what?" I finally asked out loud, not really believing — and definitely hoping it wasn't going to happen — that I'd get an answer.

"Bid higher than anyone else and low enough to cut a clean profit," the voice echoed around me in the enclosed car. "You should know that much by now." Only Max could talk that loud.

Instinct had always worked for me and suddenly I knew exactly what to do. I grabbed the cap off my head and tossed it to the far corner of the floor on the passenger's side.

"How much higher?" I asked, catching a glimpse of my wild eyes in the rear view mirror. I also had my fingers crossed and my knees braced against the steering wheel post to keep them from knocking. There was no answer. I cleared my throat, realizing my voice was barely audible and maybe I should speak up. "How much higher?" Still, no answer.

Looking at the cap, snap brim facing me and smooth crown line looking as sleek as a sports car, took all of my nerve. Reaching for it and actually holding it took more courage than I thought I had but I finally held it in my shaking hands. "How much higher?" I tried again.

"Figure Hank will go in at a c-note per, and the other guys will bid pretty much the same. Hank, though, will offer points on everything taken in over one and a half, and he's got a good enough reputation to maybe pull it off. He'll move most of them for about one and three quarters and kick back another couple of c-notes when he's done in about a month, clearing over two grand."

The statement was made so quickly and so matter-of-factly that this time not only didn't I have time to get the creepies but I was even ready with my next question.

"So what do I bid?"

"More cash up front and pay off quicker. Come in at one and a quarter for the entire drop."

I figured it out as best I could while sitting in a darkened car talking to I wasn't sure who.

"Okay, that's five kay up front for maybe two later. But I haven't got the five."

The car was silent. I wasn't scared any more. Now I was anxious. I mean, I got used to the idea pretty quick of Max talking to me but now if he wasn't talking to me, why? Bringing the cap I was still holding at arms length closer, I waited. Nothing. Taking a deep breath I plunged right in and put the cap back on my head.

The shout nearly deafened me.

"After twenty years with me if you don't think you can get trust on half the load, and that's only twenty sets, for less than a week, you don't think at all."

"Oh, yeah," I replied meekly. "I wasn't thinking."

After what was a welcome pause, giving my ringing ears a rest, the next communication was almost gentle.

"Listen kid, Charley, my friend, I want to look out for you but I don't know how long I can. You've gotta start thinking. I know that anyone who can use a mouth the way you do has got to have something going on behind the mouth."

"Okay, half on spec and payment in full before the second half. I know I can move them on the streets, I think." Feeling pretty satisfied with myself, I sat there thinking about my very first, my very own, deal.

"Uhh, by the way," I finally asked when the glow started to

wear off and the curiosity returned, "is that really you, Max?"

I decided to wear ear plugs whenever I wore the cap after the next answer. He came through, loud — which is an understatement — and clear.

"No, you idiot. It's the blinking tooth fairy."

WHEN I got home my wife was waiting for me with mascara-streaked eyes. I knew something was very wrong. Dotty would never let herself be seen, even by me, looking like that. It was her defense against the extra fifty pounds she'd put on after we were married — the eyelashes had to be perfect 24-hours a day. The hospital had called. Max was dead. He died just minutes after I left the room and, my mind boggled at the thought, probably before I'd put his cap on.

Dotty liked Max a lot. He'd taken care of both of us when we first got married, almost like the father neither one of us had. If we'd have had kids he would have thought them his own flesh and blood, but we didn't. Almost, and Dotty remembers how Max made sure she had the best doctors and best care. He even sent a big bunch of different colored carnations every day — it was the only flower he ever sent — and brought her a feathered bed jacket to cheer her up. It hadn't cheered her up much, not then, but she never forgot what Max did.

I held his cap in my hands as they lowered Max into the ground. He didn't have anything to say that day, but I knew what I had to do.

THE video recorder deal went off as planned. Even better really, 'cause it seemed none of the guys expected me to bid, much less win. Maybe they'd thought I'd be in mourning or that I was just Max's lackey — running errands, getting coffee, picking up his girl friends. But they forgot I was also his friend. And Max always did look out for his own.

After that things pretty much settled down and we were back to business as usual. Sitting around, drinking and dealing — cards that is — waiting to hear what was going to hit the streets next. In good times, a truck a week could lose its load to the streets. When it was slow, a few weeks would go by in between contracts.

It was slow, which left us a lot of time to sit around and kill. Hank and the guys that hung around him started to talk about taking over. That was okay because the guys that hung around me talked about the same thing.

I had Pete and Mike on my side, and I felt pretty good about that. Pete was one of the older guys who'd been a close second to Max. Now Pete got the idea that I really was the one behind all of Max's winning bids and it didn't hurt my reputation to let him keep talking that way. Mike was young and new to the club, but he was as tough as they came. He was also pretty close mouthed, which I liked. It cut down the competition to get a word in edgewise.

Hank had always been followed like glue by Dave and Sam and they seemed to stick even closer to him now that he was talking about being number one. Dave and Sam were brothers who, in my opinion, didn't share one brain between them. Unfortunately, they had enough brawn for an entire defensive line.

EVERYTHING was holding its own until Sugar Joe showed up at the club and sat down at Hank's table.

Sugar Joe looked a lot older now than he did five years ago. His retirement had set deep lines in his face and curved his back so that now he walked with a cane. That cane was mean looking. The hand grip was the head of a dog with its carved teeth bared and the whole thing seemed pretty hefty for a frail old guy to use. What really got to me were the side looks that Joe kept slipping my table. His eyes were the only part of him that hadn't aged. They were as bright and sharp as ever and maybe just as filled with hate.

Pete and Mike didn't seem bothered by the looks but I was the only one sitting with a view to catch them all. Plus they hadn't seen the hate in Joe's eyes from behind the barrel of a gun — one that was pointed at them. Mike sat in my old seat and Pete picked the one to my left to christen as his. You know where I sat. It was the only chair in a corner with a view of the entire room.

Using his cane, Sugar Joe shuffled over to stand by our table. The club was pretty full and the one thing I figured was there wouldn't be any trouble.

"I haven't forgotten you," Joe said as he wagged his finger at me. "Your big mouth saved Max's butt that day but now you gotta worry about who's going to save yours."

"From what, Joe?" I calmly responded. I couldn't believe this old geezer was really threatening me in front of the entire club but, despite my coolness, my knees were threatening to act like castanets. It doesn't take much strength to pull a trigger.

His wheezy laugh silenced the club room.

"Not from me, that's for sure." Before I could act the wise guy and agree with him, Joe continued.

"You think you're sitting on top now, but wait. One deal you've made, that's it. That's all you had and that's all you're going to get. Max's last words probably were telling you how to handle the deal, but he ain't around and you haven't got the smarts to figure it out."

Pete jumped up, pushing his chair back so that it fell over with a loud crash. "Hey, old man, you haven't been around in a long time. What do you know. It's Charley here that's been the brains for some time now, or didn't you know?"

Guys were slipping out of the club room pretty quick. Not like the old days when the smell of trouble would be bringing them in from the streets instead of sending them out.

Joe's cackle laugh started again. "This pup, the brains? Yeah, and I'm the tooth fairy."

His crack reminded me that I hadn't heard from Max since before his funeral. As I reached up to touch the cap, Joe's eyes followed my movements. His weird laugh again filled the now almost empty room.

"You think the world revolves around this club house. Well, I haven't been here in years and my world's grown pretty big." I figured Joe was acting a little off the wall, but he kept right on ranting, getting himself more and more worked up.

"There are lot of other deals going down in town, deals you know nothing about. Your little part, the part the boys let you have, is all you know. I've been out there," Joe said and waved his nasty looking cane in the general direction of the men's room, "and let me tell you, you young punk, you ain't been no-where."

To be honest, Sugar Joe left me speechless. Me. I didn't know what he was talking about. Pete saved the day for me by hooting a laugh at Sugar Joe and announcing "it's all a crock" to the room at large. Then Pete pulled out a deck of cards and passed them to me to cut. Sugar Joe looked as us for awhile with a twisted little grin on his face but finally he hobbled away to sit down with Hank, Dave, and Sam.

The four of them sat with their heads together, whispering up a storm. Every once in awhile I caught Joe slipping me that look but I was holding winning cards and didn't pay much attention. We played until late and locked up as we left. Everyone else had long gone.

HITTING the street, I breathed in the fresh cool air trying to clear out some of the stale cigar smoke I'd been inhaling for hours. My car was a block away and, slipping my cap forward — I knew it looked sharp like that — I sauntered down the block to the Caddy. Yeah, I got the car. Max's daughter was glad to have the two grand I made on the deal plus I threw in some of the other stuff that Max didn't tell me exactly what to do with.

The sleek lines of the jet black coach waited for me on the corner. I still couldn't believe it was all mine. Carefully opening the door, so as not to scratch the perfect finish, the new leather luxury perfume greeted me like a kiss. I slid into the soft bucket seat and quietly sat, enjoying the moment.

I hadn't heard from Max in two weeks now but, until tonight, I'd been too busy wheeling and dealing to give it much thought. Sugar Joe's mentioning the tooth fairy had reminded me of Max. There'd been something else he said, too, but I couldn't quite pin it down.

The streets were deserted and the locked Caddy gave me a feeling of peace and security. Adjusting the cap on my head, I screwed my eyes tightly closed and thought as hard as I could about Max. I must have sat there for a half an hour, trying over and over again, but nothing happened.

Feeling weary and knowing that I should have been between the sheets hours ago, I reached for the keys to start the car. Keeping quiet for as long as I had was tiring. "Max," I said out loud, "I guess you ain't coming back any more. I'm going to miss you, old pal." Unfortunately, I wasn't wearing the ear plugs. The yell almost knocked the Caddy's keys out of my hands.

"You creep! All you could send for my funeral was a lousy bunch of some weird flower. They were deader than me! Why couldn't you send something classy, like carnations."

"Max, I'm sorry," I almost sobbed, both out of relief that Max was still there and from fear that he was upset. "I was broke and Ned the florist wouldn't give me credit. They were nice flowers. They were mums. Ned said you liked them."

A few minutes silence passed and I got nervous again. Maybe Max was mad at me and had finally left me for good.

"Ahh, forget the flowers. They were okay. I was just looking forward to some nice carnations, maybe purple ones. Always wanted to have purple carnations at my funeral. Classy, you know."

Breathing a sigh of relief that Max seemed appeased, I jiggled the car keys in my hand wondering, whether or not to start up the car. Did Max notice I was driving his Caddy? Could he see? Or just talk to me? I'd never thought it all the way through and now I worried a bit that he might not like my having the car.

"I see you got the Caddy, Charley," the voice said pleasantly. Now I wondered if he could read minds. Not that I had anything to hide from Max, I just wasn't sure I liked the idea of someone knowing what I was thinking. "I guess you took care of the kid," he continued, and that put me at ease — knowing that he didn't actually know.

"I gave her the take from the contract, Max, plus the silver stuff and the sound system. She said she'd rather keep the wagon."

"I'm not surprised. It's like that Gucci bag she carries, the thing that looks like a satchel. It must hold half her medicine cabinet. You can't get her to part with it. But everything turned out okay."

"She was real happy with the money and the silver, Max. I had to make her take the sound system, I mean, I just didn't feel right," my voice trailed off, "uhh, is that what you mean, Max?"

"I meant with the contract," he sounded like he was losing his patience. "You had the two grand so it must have gone good."

"Yeah, just like you said, Max."

"Why didn't you bid on the next contract, the one for all that fancy kitchen stuff?"

I didn't have an answer I knew he would buy, so I tried to think real fast. The real reason was that I didn't know what to bid so I told the guys I wanted to take it easy for a while. I didn't want to tell Max that, so I finally said, "Oh, that fancy kitchen stuff. Well, I didn't think there was much of a market for it. I mean, no one I know uses a cuissy-whatis. Even Dotty didn't want one."

"Yeah, Charley, I should have known that would be a bit much to ask. What about the contract coming up — what are you going to bid?"

"Uhh, what contract?" If Max couldn't read minds, how come he always knew what was going on?

The roar really hurt my ears. I reminded myself to take the ear plugs from my night table and have them handy for Max's next chat.

"Don't you keep track of anything? There's a load of game computers that just fell off a truck in New Jersey. They should be here in a day or two. What are you going to bid?"

Game computers, I thought to myself. What do I do with game computers? I'd no idea what they sold for — hot or cold.

"Uhh, Max, what do you think I should do?" I asked this with just the right note, I hoped, of confidence. You know, like I really knew what to do but was just checking. I don't think it worked.

"I should have known you couldn't move without me," he sighed, "even though you got the boys to say you've been working my contracts for years. I should have known."

This surprised me. Of course Max knew I didn't move without him.

"Max, things just don't change overnight. I mean, if you help out a few times then maybe I'll be able to go it on my own. I'm just not used to working without you, that's all."

"Okay, Charley, I'll help you out this time. The game computers are mostly Commodore's, cold price of about $200. You can move them out pretty easy at one and a quarter." He sighed again. "Maybe you'd better not try points and stuff just yet, just go for an up front dollar."

"How about I bid seventy-five each, Max. That sounds pretty good."

"It's going to sound good to all the other guys bidding the same price. You've got to be different. Hank'll probably come in with seventy-five plus points. Go high, kid. For now at least it'll get you the contract."

"How high, Max?"

I took the silence that followed to be Max thinking of a good price. It wasn't. He was upset with me, again.

"As high as you want, just get the contract," he said and while it wasn't quite loud enough to hurt I began to worry about someone passing by, overhearing. I could always say I was a ventriloquist. Maybe I should keep a dummy in the car. I was about to share this thought with Max when I realized what his comment would be so I kept it to myself.

There was welcome quiet for awhile before he softly continued. "Try eighty-five, Charley, try eighty-five."

I decided not to ask Max about the up front money, hoping that the deal I worked last time for half the goods up front could be repeated. Instead, I got curious again.

"Max, uhh, how is it where, well, where you are?"

You could hear the merriment in his voice. "It's just fine, Charley, just fine. Lot's of long leggy blondes."

Wherever he was sounded pretty good to me, although I wasn't in any big hurry to join him. I figured it was time to grab some shut eye so, wishing Max a good night, I headed home.

THE bid turned out just like he said. Three of the loners from the club teamed up to bid eighty, half the goods on credit, and Hank came in at seventy-five plus points. Hank would have gotten it, except for my bid at eighty-five. I got the advance credit and then when the middle man, Sid, shook my hand on the deal, Hank glowered. Sugar Joe didn't look to happy either, but he had a strange twist to his mouth that I couldn't quite pin down to losing the contract.

The first half of the load went like hot-cakes. It seems that the kids at home were clamoring to play these weird knights-in-shining-armor games and had been begging and bugging their folks to distraction. They practically lined up on the street. The first hundred sets moved out in less than a week.

I turned the eight grand over to Sid for the other half load. A hundred more sets and, as far as I was concerned, all paid for. All the money that came in now was mine, less overhead, of course. Pete and Mike had to be taken care of, the way Max used to take care of me, but I figured I'd clear four kay.

My garage had been seeing a lot of traffic the past week, which the neighbors might have thought was odd if they hadn't been part of the overhead. Max had taught me well. A couple of c-notes closes a lot of eyes.

Pete had just picked up three sets and secured them in the trunk of my old LTD. He'd had his eye on the LTD for awhile, and it was his cut for helping me move the video stuff. He'd turned his Pinto over to Mike. The three of us were all driving new wheels.

"Charley," Pete looked at me strangely as he spoke, "word's out on the streets to stay clear of you. Of us, really. I picked up on it in the men's room at Kelly's tavern."

I couldn't have been more surprised, everything was moving so well. "What kind of word, Pete," I asked, trying to figure out what was being said and who started it.

Leaning on the trunk of the the LTD, Pete looked as puzzled as I felt. "I caught a few words before the guys looked in the mirror and realized I was there. One of them said that something was going down this week and not to pick anything up off the street. The other guy asked what was going down, and that's when they saw me."

"Who were they?" I was curious but couldn't figure out how I fit into this.

"Just some guys that hang out at Kelly's," Pete answered. "Maybe it's nothing, but it was the way they shut up when they saw me that started me thinking."

I tipped my cap back to scratch my head. "Pete, you're seeing ghosts," I said before I realized that was my recent area of expertise.

"I mean, what they were saying didn't have anything to do with us. How could it? Everything's cool."

"Yeah, you're right," Pete agreed before he started up the LTD. He'd had the points cleaned and it purred like new. "Just thought I'd mention it."

"See you later, Pete, we still got a lot of work to do," I warned him — thinking maybe he was trying to get some time off by getting me to slow down sales — and waved him off. Locking the garage door, with the 97 computers behind it, I turned to go into the house.

Four black and white police cars pulled up in front of my house and emptied the cops inside before I was halfway to the back door. Guns drawn, eight cops closed in around me. Still holding the garage key in my hand I was frozen to the spot, speechless.

"Hold it right there," a voice rang out from one of the cops, as if I could even think of going anywhere else. The Caddy was parked on the other side of the black and whites and Pete was long gone. "Check the garage," the same voice ordered one of the other cops, who managed to get the key from my clenched fist without even asking. "If the garage is holding what we think, you're under arrest."

It did and I was.

"Max, what do I do?" I whispered as they cuffed me.

"This ain't Max, Charley, it's the tooth fairy, like I said." The voice must have been heard by the cop leading me to his black and white, but he didn't seem to notice.

"I had Max's cap bugged months ago to keep tabs on him. Like I said, Charley, you ain't got no idea what's going on in the rest of the world. Like micro-chip receivers, transmitters and amplifiers."

I finally recognized the voice and it all fell into place. "Sugar Joe."

"The one and only. It took me years to figure out how to get back at Max, except he died first. You were a sweet second in line for revenge. And I got it — setting you up for a fall. Signing off, Charley, I ain't going to be broadcasting for awhile."

It didn't do me any good to really know why "Max" had gotten me the contracts — there was no way to set me up unless I was caught dealing and Sugar Joe even had to help me do that.

I'd end up with four years away, room and board included, time enough to figure out what to do next. Maybe, if they let me keep the cap, I could really get in touch with Max. He'd know what to do, I mumbled.

"I do, Charley, I do."   ✗

A Reputation for Murder
by M.J. Elliott

I'M getting to the age where one can be quite forgetful about some things but not about others. I never leave taps running, for instance, but I often get into the bath only to discover that I didn't put the plug in. I don't recall, therefore, whether I told you about my first murder case in Overdale. If I haven't, then there's precious little point now, since I'm about to reveal the identity of the murderer. The year was . . . oh, goodness, I'm not sure. '31, perhaps, but if you were to tie me down and threaten me with a branding iron I couldn't swear to it. I'm reasonably content that it was late summer — I recollect the sort of peaceful evenings for which the word "charming" was created.

I'm not in the habit of cutting long stories short — quite the opposite, in fact — but I'm prepared to give it a try so that we can get on to the poisoning of the Reverend Parbold in good time. I trust I'm not inflating my ego to bursting point if I assume that you're all quite familiar with the ingredients of a traditional Hilary Caine murder mystery; and believe me, this one was no different: packed off to the aforementioned Yorkshire hamlet of Overdale by the editors of *Tittle Tattle* Magazine (for whom I occupied the vaguely-defined position of "Detective in Residence") in order to solve a crime that had, up to that point, baffled the local police. It was the old story of a crime of passionlessness (if there is such a word) and an ingeniously concocted alibi. Breaking it didn't cause me too much hardship, but the arrest of Major Stuart-Davies did cause something of a stir in the village. So impressed were the locals with my display of ratiocination and so pleased were they to see the back of the Major, that I understand there was even talk of commissioning a statue in my honour. The suggestion had been dismissed almost immediately on the grounds of cost and pointlessness; but since I never got so much as a bouquet of flowers for solving a crime in London, I was at least glad of the sentiment.

But the biggest reward I received from the case was the friendship of the local police inspector, Paddy Troughton, a good-hearted chap with a face like a crumpled-up paper bag, and a lazy eye to boot. To say that I assisted him on the case would be to misrepresent our working relationship. In fact, to describe it as a *working* relationship would be just as much of a misrepresentation; he more or less turned proceedings over to me and stood in the background, waiting to slap the handcuffs on someone. "Having you down here has been the closest thing to a holiday I've had since 1923," he explained after the business was concluded. I made the mistake of asking him what happened in 1923. "I buried the wife," he replied, stopping the conversation in its tracks.

Anyway, the case had been solved; the Major had been arrested; and, barring the unlikely event that I would be required to give testimony at the trial, my involvement was at an end and I was preparing to leave Overdale for good. I'd been using Inspector Troughton's spare room, so taken with me was he by that stage, and I had decided to leave him a few back issues of *Tittle Tattle* as a sort of goodbye present. Yes, I know I complain about them; but they do at least write consistently nice things about me; and their artists, bless their nibs, always draw me at least two dress sizes smaller than I really am.

TROUGHTON was already getting stuck in before I was even out of the door. People have this habit of reading the stories back to me, as if to gauge my reaction, and I'm sorry to have to report that the Inspector was no different.

" 'Voila!' cried Hilary Caine with a dramatic flourish: 'The only way Lord Greyhaven could have appeared at the scene of the murder and at his anniversary party in Monte Carlo at the same time — with the assistance of his identical twin brother, Roland!' "

I emitted a small sigh. "Actually, his name was *Ronald,*" I admitted, "and he wasn't a twin, he was a cousin with a strong family resemblance. And I've never said 'Voila!,' much less done anything with a dramatic flourish."

He lowered the magazine. "Why are the policemen in your stories always such dullards, Miss Caine?" he asked.

Ah, the old sweet song.

"Don't take it to heart, Inspector. It's my job to identify the criminals, but I don't write their wrongs, so to speak."

"Perhaps you should complain to the publishers," he suggested.

I smiled my most becoming smile and explained that I had given up trying many years ago (not that I remember trying all that hard in the first place) and that details were frequently exaggerated in the interest of sales.

Satisfied with my unsatisfactory explanation, he perused

the publication once more. "I must say, it makes quite a change from the parish newsletter. And you're their . . . what do you call yourself . . . 'Girl Detective'?"

"I don't call myself anything of the sort, Inspector. But as I'm sure you've noticed, I do have a certain instinct in that direction. So they contact me whenever a noteworthy crime appears to have mislaid its solution, and I reunite the two."

Troughton frowned, and as he did so his eyes nearly disappeared into his heavily wrinkled face. "And that doesn't seem . . . *vulgar* to you at all, Miss Caine?"

I fancy I may also have frowned at this point although I doubt that the effect would have been anywhere near as startling. But if the moment of my departure from Overdale was to be an excuse for blunt talk, then I could be as blunt as the best of them. "Being poor seems vulgar to me, Inspector," I said flatly. "And I'd sooner saw off my own extremities with a rusty bread knife than go begging to my father. In any case, my arrangement with them is purely temporary, you understand. I could give up any time I wanted. I could. I'm just tapering off gradually. And one meets the most interesting people. Occasionally, one arrests them. But on the whole, my most agreeable acquaintances have been on the right side of the law."

This seemed to bring the discussion back into a more relaxed arena, and I recognised that fatherly smile upon Troughton's face once more. When I say "fatherly," by the way, I don't include my own father in that category.

"Well, I certainly can't complain," he said. "I'd never have picked Major Stuart-Davies out as a killer, not in a million years. You're sure we can't persuade you to stay in Overdale one more week?"

This was a most unexpected invitation — I wasn't aware then that there was a 'we' who felt so strongly about my presence.

"No, I'm afraid my work here is done," I replied, enjoying some satisfaction at finally being able to say that phrase out loud.

"Well, I know there'll be plenty who'll miss you, Miss Caine. Folk are starting to look on you as quite a fixture." Perhaps that was the thinking behind the statue suggestion, who can say? "I'd even go so far as to say you've become the toast of the village."

At more or less that moment, a toast was indeed being proposed in Overdale, but wouldn't you know it, I was not the toastee, although my name did come into the conversation and remain there for quite some time. Please store that fact in a safe place — we may require it later on. The toast was in honour of the lovely Miss Elspeth Seagrave and it was performed with tea rather than champagne, but I have no doubt of the toaster's sincerity. Claude Mountjoy had an appalling habit of only ever saying what he thought — which, of course, always means social suicide — and if he claimed to wish Miss Seagrave well, then I must take it that he did indeed wish her well. Her uncle, the Reverend Alistair Parbold, however, Mountjoy did not wish well, and so he took delight in goading the old man whenever the opportunity arose. I understand, for instance, that the question, "Haven't you got anything stronger than tea? Communion wine, for instance?" passed Claude's lips fairly early on in the proceedings.

Parbold would not be goaded — not at this stage in the proceedings, at any rate. Elspeth probably giggled and told Mountjoy how terrible he was. Jago Meridian would have said nothing.

Anyway, to get back to matters of which I have definite first-hand knowledge, I had just finished off my goodbye cup of tea, and decided that the time had finally come to actually *say* goodbye.

"Well, I should really be off now," I said. "Duty calls and all that rot."

"Don't you think Scotland Yard can cope with the London criminal in your absence, Miss Caine?" Troughton asked.

"Oh, they're all right in a pinch, but I don't like to leave them unsupervised for too long. I left instructions for Inspector Finn to be walked twice a day; but if I'm away for more than a week, he starts to pine. Besides, in a village the size of Overdale, I should think one murder's your lot for the next decade or so."

And at more or less that moment . . . well, I think you can guess, can't you? Fate can be cruel, but it needn't enjoy itself quite so much.

I finished packing, and was just on the brink of asking whether a police escort to the railway station might not be out of the question, when the telephone rang. As Troughton listened to the person on the other end of the line, I could tell that something was very wrong. His face didn't go grey; given that his complexion was bright red for most of the time, so I doubt that it *could*. But I daresay the level of redness in his cheeks decreased at the news.

"The Vicarage? Good God! Hold the fort, Sergeant."

Without speaking, I returned to my room and began unpacking.

I never really considered Jane Marple serious competition in the detecting stakes — probably mean-spirited of me, but she always struck me as pretty small fry — but for years after this investigation, I had to put up with all kinds of talk from ignorant people who imagined that I'd 'borrowed' the notion of a murder at the vicarage from the old biddy. In fact, I was ahead of her by about a year. Perhaps not quite a year, but definitely a good few months. I'm certain that I remember travelling by train somewhere and reading about the St. Mary Mead business in the newspaper and feeling a certain satisfaction that I had been there first. I was the Roald Amundsen of detection, if you like.

UPON arrival at the Vicarage, I was really more interested in the late Reverend Alistair Parbold than in talking to the suspects, a job I left to Inspector Troughton. Poisoning cases can be such a bind; in ninety percent of the cases, you're left hanging until some test-tube johnny identifies the fatal substance — that's if it's ever identified, since poison dissipates in the body a lot sooner than Reggie Fortune or Roger Sheringham would have you imagine.

Parbold lay where he had fallen by the dining room table. The late summer sun helped to make the majority of the scene quite a picturesque affair. As I think you've gathered by now, I had quite a reputation by this stage, and my finer sensibilities were no longer affected by the possibility of a corpse spoiling the ambience. And as ambiences go, this one was more than usually pleasurable: a spacious room with plenty of windows giving out onto a well-tended lawn. So there was no possibility that a rogue poisoner could just have sneaked up on the proceedings without being spotted by the revellers. I gave everything on the table an experimental sniff, in the unlikely event that the poison might reveal itself to my nasal passages. But only the odour of tea and potted meat sandwiches made itself clear. I noticed in passing that one of the four people present that afternoon preferred lemon in his tea to milk.

Some sensitive and respectful soul — the police sergeant, perhaps — had placed a napkin over Parbold's face. I removed it and began my examination, silently giving thanks as I did so for the fact that tea, not alcohol, had been consumed that afternoon. There might after all still be a chance of ascertaining what the killer had used to achieve this result if right-thinking people acted quickly. The purple blotches on the victim's face grabbed my attention immediately. I trust I don't have to tell you what they signified. Or do I? Did I ever tell you about the poisoning of Brigadier General La Frenais during a regimental dinner? I didn't? Oh, well — another time, perhaps.

I arrived in the hallway just as Inspector Troughton was closing the front door on the slim back of a young man. I pointed a finger and raised an eyebrow — the international sign for 'Who was that?'

"Young Mr Meridian. I took his statement and told him he could go home. Sergeant Bates is seeing — er, taking Mr Mountjoy back right now."

I wondered whether this Mountjoy was particularly frail, particularly wealthy, or particularly suspicious to merit such attention.

"Out of curiosity," I asked, "did either of them mention anything about violent spasms? From the Reverend, I mean."

"Both of them, as it happens. Haven't had a proper talk with Miss Seagrave yet — she wanted to be left alone in the morning room to collect her thoughts — but I have no doubt she'll say the same. It's important, I take it?"

"Well, sad to say, I know more about poisons than any well-brought up girl my age should, and I think I can hazard a guess as to what was used. I recommend your police doctor checks his findings with a chap in London called Quigley, but I'd say the killer used something in the Datora family. It's nasty stuff — and quick. There *is* an antidote, I understand."

"Be a bit late in this case," observed Troughton. He had a point: I suspect I was just showing off. To hide my shame, I asked if I could be allowed to participate in the questioning of the dead man's niece, not that there would ever have been any doubt of that, of course.

Yes, Elspeth Seagrave was beautiful. Not beautiful like Vanessa Baxendale-Moroney (don't worry about having to remember the name; it was a different case entirely), but clearly the sort of young woman who could go out in all weathers and still appear fresh and unblemished, blast her. Perhaps if our investigations hadn't been taking place in a vicarage, I might have asked God to ensure that she would turn out to be the killer.

She was also, as one might expect, highly emotional, what with having recently seen her uncle die a horrible and unnatural death and all. I don't want you to come away with the impression that I'm at all intolerant of people's feelings at such a traumatic time; I'm just not awfully good at dealing with them.

Introductions were as awkward as one might expect under

the circumstances, and Elspeth's eyes flashed at the mention of my name.

"Hilary Caine, of course," she said, through the sobs. "We were all talking about you . . . before Uncle . . . before he . . ."

There's nothing worse than being forced to take frequent breaks during an interrogation in order to allow the tears to flow freely, as I had the feeling they were about to, so I jumped in with the first thing I could think to say, no matter how banal.

"You're American, I think." The Great Detective at work.

"From Boston," she confirmed with a sniff. "My mother was Uncle's sister."

I took the past tense as an indication. "Your mother's dead?"

She nodded. "Father, too. Uncle Alistair was my last living — I mean . . ."

I felt another sob coming on, and I didn't really think that I could avert it with another statement of the painfully obvious. Troughton had, as per usual, positioned himself by the door with the apparent intention of keeping out of things, so I hoped to cause a distraction by bringing him into the conversation.

"Was the vicar married, Inspector?" I asked. I was reasonably certain that vicars were permitted to marry, but unsure whether it was mandatory.

"No, Miss Caine."

"Very wise. Didn't Sherlock Holmes say 'women are never to be entirely trusted, not even the best of them'? He was right, you know."

"And do you include yourself in that?" he asked.

"Oh, absolutely! That's why I make a point of going through my pockets late at night. I met him once, you know, Sherlock Holmes. Small feet."

Elspeth, evidently of the opinion that her finer feelings were not being addressed, began to weep once more. After attempting to offer some few words of condolence, with, unsurprisingly, little success, I decided to press on in any event.

"So, Miss Seagrave, the Reverend Parbold: he was your only liv— er, remaining relative."

She nodded.

"And you were his."

"Well . . . naturally."

"So . . . you'd be his sole heir, then."

Elspeth gave a last sniff. "I guess so. I've never thought about it."

"Was he a wealthy man?"

"I've really no idea."

Again, I looked to our silent friend the Inspector for clarification.

"The Parbolds were the local squires a generation ago," he answered. "I can't see that the Reverend would have spent all their wealth. He was a man of simple tastes. Didn't even employ a housekeeper."

No housekeeper . . . "So who prepared lunch today?"

"Oh, *he* did," Elspeth answered, now seeming somewhat brighter. "I offered, but he said this was my last day in the country, I should be waited upon." She paused. "I suppose I'll have to stay a little longer now."

"For the funeral, you mean?" I asked, and instantly wished I hadn't. Once more, the floodgates opened and there was nothing for me to do but wait and supply the occasional "there, there." Eventually, she calmed down enough for me to be able to ask about the other guests at the luncheon.

"Just a couple of friends I made during my stay here. Claude Mountjoy. Oh, and Jago, of course."

"Mr Meridian: church organist." This contribution courtesy of Inspector Troughton, anticipating my next question. So the thin young gentleman I had seen escorted off the premises a short time ago was "Jago" to Miss Seagrave.

"And what did lunch consist of?"

Elspeth gave a gentle shrug. It was very becoming, unlike my own shrugs — don't get me started. "Just tea and sandwiches," she answered.

"Paste sandwiches, weren't they?" I asked. "Meat or fish, do you recall? I had a quick sniff but I couldn't tell by smell alone."

"I'm afraid it all tastes the same to me."

That seemed fair enough. They all smelled the same to me, too, so there was no good reason why they all shouldn't taste the same. "And did everyone have sandwiches?"

"Sure, I think. Oh wait, I don't think Jago had anything to eat. But there can't have been anything in them — I mean, *I* had a bite." She looked pleadingly at the Inspector, as though that would have done any good. "And Claude was the first one to eat. He practically ate one whole — jammed the thing into his mouth and spat crumbs everywhere when he spoke."

He sounded like someone you'd love to introduce to mother. "Hungry, was he?"

"I think he just did it to annoy Uncle."

If Inspector Troughton found this suggestion of enmity between Mountjoy and Parbold interesting, he gave no sign of it. "They didn't get on?" I enquired.

Elspeth bestowed a wan smile upon us. "I guess not. I didn't realise 'til today. I thought Uncle was friends with everyone. But during lunch something happened — I don't know for certain what caused it, whether it was Claude spitting food, or when he said that they should have poured some communion wine to toast me properly, but when he thought I couldn't hear him, Uncle leaned in close to Claude and whispered: 'I'll thank you to mind your manners, Mountjoy. May I remind you that you are here on sufferance.'

"Claude smiled, and replied: 'An act of martyrdom that will doubtless stand you in good stead when you stand, at last, on the threshold of the afterlife.'

" 'Is that a threat?' asked Uncle.

" 'Heaven forbid,' Claude replied."

"And then?" I asked.

"Nothing. We all began to talk about the recent goings on in Overdale, and then —" She halted.

"And you're certain that's what was said, Miss Seagrave? Even though it was a whispered conversation?" Troughton seemed to have come to life once more.

Elspeth nodded vigorously. "I have very acute hearing, Inspector. The doctors back home say I'm a real marvel."

I hoped this young lady's memory would prove as reliable as her hearing.

"Do you recall whether everyone drank their tea, Elspeth?" I asked.

She bit her lip. A bad sign. "I think so."

"Think so or know so?"

A nod this time. "I'm sure of it, yes. We all drank. I've always liked tea. Must be the English side of me."

"And did everyone take milk and sugar?"

"Oh, I don't have sugar. And Uncle prefers — *preferred* a slice of lemon in his tea. But Jago had milk and maybe one sugar. And I poured Claude's milk for him."

"No sugar for Claude?"

"Oh, he loaded the cup with it. You should have seen Uncle's expression."

Claude Mountjoy and the Reverend again . . . At least I knew what my next act should be, and whom I would have to interview. As for the above-mentioned preferences in tea-taking, I didn't have a hope in the hereafter of remembering it all, so I acquired a page from the notebook of Inspector

Troughton — who hadn't used it at all thus far in the proceedings — and wrote the following:

Claude Mountjoy — milk and sugar
Jago Meridian — milk and sugar
Elspeth Seagrave — milk, no sugar
Rev Parbold (Dec'd) — no milk/sugar, <u>slice of lemon</u>

"Is it that important?" Elspeth asked.

"I have absolutely no idea," I confessed. I looked at what I
had just written, and observed that I had underlined *"slice of
lemon"* with some vigour. Clearly, I considered it important,
and who am I to argue with myself? Looking up, I asked: "Did
your uncle slice the lemon or did someone else do it for him?"

She seemed perplexed, bless her heart. "I guess so. I mean,
I didn't see him do it." You'll notice that she knew better than
to ask me whether it might be important this time, although
for the first time since the case had begun (not so terribly long
ago, I admit), I felt that I was on the right track. Rising, I
asked Troughton if I might have a private word in the kitchen.

I thought I might get away with a polite nod in Elspeth's
direction, but it was not to be. She took my hand — a gesture
I've always been less than comfortable with — and said sincerely: "I — I just want to say I'm sorry I didn't get to know you
before all this unpleasantness. I'm sure we'd have been great
friends."

Well, what can one say to *that?* I said that I was equally
sure that would have been the case, freed myself from her grip
and scurried into the kitchen, where I discovered the Inspector
waiting for me.

"WELL, Miss Caine?" was all he seemed inclined to say.

"She is both pretty and charming," I observed. "I therefore
hate her."

Troughton raised an eyebrow.

"It's a woman's prerogative to hate any woman prettier
and more charming than she is."

"I see," he said, although I doubt that he did. "But do you
think she poisoned her uncle?" he went on.

"I've heard nothing to suggest that so far. But wouldn't it
be wonderful if she had?"

For some reason, he didn't seem to share my glee at that
prospect. Men are such illogical creatures, don't you find?

"Any other thoughts?" he asked.

I indicated the lemon from which Parbold had extracted the slice currently floating on the dregs of his tea. "I'd get that looked at," I suggested.

Despite his somewhat irksome unwillingness to participate in the interviewing of Elspeth Seagrave, Troughton's faculties were in no way dimmed. He understood what I was talking about instantly.

"I'd also like to have a chat with Claude Mountjoy, the man with the appalling table manners," I added. "I'd very much like to hear the story behind his little spat with the Reverend."

Troughton shook his head. "I think we can eliminate him as a suspect, Miss Caine."

I hate it when I feel that someone is suddenly leagues ahead of me, and I felt it right then.

"I wish I shared your certainty, Inspector. Just why can't he be our poisoner?"

"Because Claude Mountjoy is blind, Miss Caine," he replied.

Of course, you don't imagine for a minute that I would let a little bombshell like that prevent me from questioning Mountjoy. My old friend Mr Carrados didn't let his blindness prevent him from investigating a good many murders. Pursuing that notion to its logical conclusion, there was no reason why Claude Mountjoy should allow the same condition to prevent him from committing one. But there was only one way to know for certain, of course, and that was to have a chat with the man himself. Unsurprisingly, I couldn't persuade Inspector Troughton to accompany me. He'd somehow got hold of a copy of the latest *Tittle Tattle* and had decided instead to catch up on his reading, assuring me that I would do a perfectly competent job without him. Of that fact I had no doubt, arrogant young so-and-so that I was; but I was nevertheless disappointed with his lack of enthusiasm for my chosen line of inquiry.

WHEN I visited Claude Mountjoy's home, Abaddon Cottage, I discovered him pottering about in his garden, clipping protuberances from his rose bushes and dropping them into a bucket. He was not a tall man, but wide. And his grizzly ginger beard gave the impression that his face widened at the bottom.

He assured me that he was perfectly delighted to see me (yes, he said 'see'), but I must say, I had no sense of this alleged enthusiasm in his tone of voice, or in the fact that he resumed tending to his roses rather than invite me into his cottage for a cup of tea. Not that I would have accepted, given recent events, but it was an odd omission. Mr Mountjoy was no gentleman.

"Are my roses beautiful, Miss Caine?" he asked in an almost effeminate tone. Peter Lorre hadn't made it to Hollywood at this stage, but if I had to compare Claude Mountjoy to anybody, it would be him. Or do I mean 'he'?

"You're asking the wrong girl, Mr Mountjoy," I replied. "I'm afraid I've never understood the appeal of flowers."

He sighed, rising to his feet. "Such a disheartening attitude in one so young."

"Who says I'm young?"

"Your voice. You are . . . twenty-three?"

I was actually twenty-four, so I felt he deserved my congratulations.

"When one is without sight, one learns to appreciate beauty in other ways: smell, texture."

I couldn't resist the opportunity to create a little disharmony at this point, but then I rarely can. " 'God's great work,' the Reverend would have said."

Mountjoy was not so easily baited. "One does not need to imagine a controlling force behind everything in order to appreciate it. Are you by any chance a religious person?"

"I'm a lapsed cynic."

"You have my sympathies. Supporters of organised religion have brought nothing but pain and misery upon the population. They should all be shot."

I sensed that the conversation would begin to circle the plughole were I to question the logic of his argument, so I moved on.

"Elspeth — Miss Seagrave — was telling me about some strong words that passed between yourself and the Vicar. Something about him standing on the threshold of the after-life."

Mountjoy shook his head wearily. "Dear, dear Elspeth. Such a sweet girl, but like all her sex, so painfully indiscreet. For a man who made the worship of God his profession rather than his hobby, Alistair Parbold was very easily goaded on the subject."

"And your goading upset him so?"

"I am a very, very good goader, if there is such a thing. I'm sure you'd like to know what transpired before my chiding. The conversation went along the following lines: Parbold, masking his discomfort with a thin veneer of affability, attempted to make this somewhat awkward gathering less so by starting up a conversation. I proposed 'old times' as a likely topic — a suggestion that did not meet with much enthusiasm. Miss Seagrave berated her uncle for overlooking the only topic to have held the interests of the tiny minds that make up Overdale."

I remembered that when I'd first been introduced to Elspeth and before she'd broken into the first of many floods of tears, she'd said something like, "We were all talking about you."

"You talked about the recent murder case and the arrest of Major Stuart-Davies?" I suggested.

"Naturally. Miss Seagrave said that, although she'd barely known the Major, she was surprised when he was arrested. In suitably ridiculous fashion, the Reverend agreed with her, adding: 'I'm sorry to say he pulled the wool over everyone's eyes, mine included.' I pointed out that to do so must surely be the prerogative of the lost sheep. Despite my exceedingly witty and ingenious interjection, the old man was less than amused and his temper only became worse. Really, it was worth it just to see the look on his face."

"Excuse me?" I asked, thinking for a moment that I might have misheard.

"Just an expression, Miss Caine. I'm sure you know what I mean."

I wondered whether I did know what he meant.

"So, no love lost between the two of you?" I observed, as though that point hadn't already been made abundantly clear.

Mountjoy smiled a Father Christmas smile. "I suppose it would be fair to say that I had hate in my heart for Mr Parbold," he said.

"Hate enough to kill?"

He appeared to mull this notion over. "I can't say I've ever really considered it, but . . . yes, why not?"

"Any particular reason?"

"No, no particular reason," he said, lightly.

And it seemed to me that he really meant it. He hated Alistair Parbold simply because he could.

"Most people wouldn't go to such extremes," I noted.

"Then I take great comfort in the fact that I am not most people. Please, take a turn with me around the garden. Perhaps you might come to revise your opinions."

I wondered whether the same might be true of my companion, but I doubted it very much. Nevertheless, stroll we did, and our conversation continued, interrupted only by the odd bit of Latin, Claude Mountjoy's attempt at improving my botanical knowledge.

As we walked, I asked whether his attitude regarding Parbold might not be looked upon as a trifle excessive. Mountjoy grew more animated as the conversation took a darker turn.

"Only if you believe that a system exists for measuring so-called good and evil. And before you warn me about saying as much to your friend Inspector Troughton, I should advise you that I have informed him of my opinions on more than one occasion. Law is nothing more than the crystallized prejudices of the community, Miss Caine. Everybody dies. Sooner or later, one way or another. To punish those who take life strikes me as the worst form of hypocrisy in an already hypocritical society."

"Myself, I'd like to believe there are less finite methods of solving a dispute. But then, I'm only a woman and can't be expected to think about such things logically."

He harrumphed at this; or rather, he gave a sound that is usually described as a harrumph, but doesn't really sound that way. "I can tell from your tone of voice that you don't *really* think that."

"And what *do* I really think, Mr Mountjoy?"

He started, as though he'd been on the receiving end of a sudden shock. "You surely can't believe that a helpless old blind man could have poisoned the Reverend Parbold?"

"You don't strike me as being all that helpless, or even all that old. Fifty-eight?"

He stated that he was fifty-nine, but that I was worthy of some congratulation nevertheless.

"I don't doubt that an intelligent, resourceful man with hate in his heart could accomplish anything he wanted if he put his mind to it."

"I relish the compliment. Or is it an accusation?"

I wondered about that myself.

"You're wrong about me, you know," said Mountjoy, coming to a sudden halt. He was very possibly correct, of course. I was then, and remain to this day, wrong about a good many things.

"I'm probably your most valuable witness," he continued, "since I'm the only person in Overdale who is not a hypocrite."

"Since the death of the Reverend Parbold, of course."

He smiled. "By no means. I should say that carrying on with a married parishioner would qualify as an act of hypocrisy, wouldn't you?"

I would have hated for Mountjoy to see my expression at that point, but I daresay he had anticipated my reaction. At least now I knew what he'd meant about 'old times' and why

Parbold had found it a distasteful topic for luncheon conversation. Undeterred, I pressed on. "I suppose you're too much of a gentleman to name the lady in question?" I asked.

"You suppose incorrectly, Miss Caine. The lady's name was Mrs Serena Meridian."

One could hardly forget the name Meridian in a hurry, and I remembered Elspeth's apparent fondness for the young church organist.

"And is Serena, Jago Meridian's wife?" I asked.

"His mother. I *did* say it was a somewhat awkward gathering. Did you really think that was entirely my responsibility?"

In a town the size of Overdale, there are certain people whose job it is to know everyone else's business: the elderly spinster (don't get me started on that Marple woman again), the general practitioner, and the policeman. Did I think that the indolent Inspector Troughton knew all about Parbold's affair with Serena Meridian? Oh yes. Did I want to know why he had neglected to mention this extremely pertinent detail? Oh my, yes.

UPON returning to my temporary abode, I discovered that my host was as good as his word and had spent the afternoon catching up on my adventures in the latest *Tittle Tattle.*

I related the details of my conversation with Claude Mountjoy, but I had the impression that he wasn't giving me his complete attention. I couldn't be sure, you see, whether his lazy eye wasn't scanning the pages of the publication in his lap. When I'd finished, however, he simply shook his head and said, "I don't know how you do it, Miss, I really don't."

Both eyes observed my less than gruntled expression. He sighed.

"Yes, yes, I knew," he admitted. "I was called to the Meridian place when it all came out. Victor Meridian, Jago's dad, just went berserk. Quite a temper on him."

"So what happened?" I asked.

"Well, I don't know, I haven't got to the end yet, have I?"

In frustration, I swept the magazine from his lap and right into the fireplace. Which, it being summer, wasn't lit, which is a pity, as I doubt I could have done it again if I tried.

Troughton looked up at me without a trace of shame, unless he kept it hidden under his wrinkles.

"After that little fracas, Serena broke it off with Parbold, and all seemed well again. Then six months later, Victor up and shot himself. Maybe he never really got over it, or maybe it was something else, I dunno. He always did have a rather dark, resentful side to him. Played darts with him once — he was a very poor loser. Never again."

"And how old would Jago have been at the time?"

"Oh, I can't recall, it was all so long ago. But an impressionable age. Definitely an impressionable age."

I'd always imagined that I'd had a good relationship with Troughton, but I couldn't shake the feeling now that he was making fun of me. I wondered if that had always been the case.

"What sort of an effect do you suppose a parent's suicide would have on a young boy?" I wondered aloud.

"Good question," was the reply. "P'raps you should ask him." He retrieved his copy of *Tittle Tattle* from the grate.

Frustrated by Troughton's disobliging nature, I decided to take a long walk, which might very well lead me to Jago Meridian's front door. I had known better than to ask whether the results of the examination of the lemon had arrived. Even in London, these things take an inordinate amount of time. But I continued to pin my hopes on it. After all, it was the only significant difference between Parbold's lunch and everyone else's. They'd all eaten sandwiches, hadn't they? Well, no — Jago Meridian hadn't eaten, but Elspeth and Mountjoy certainly had, and they weren't dead. No, everyone else had taken milk with his or her tea — it just had to be the lemon. I stopped for a moment, aware that a notion was tickling the back of my brain. What was it? No, gone again. I just had to hope that it would make itself known before I had to return to London. I should add that I wasn't in the least bit troubled over the issue of how the killer got his hands on a dose of Datura; it's my experience that if a person's determined enough, they can do whatever they set their mind to doing.

Jago Meridian had just prepared a pot of tea when I arrived at his home. In whichever direction I cared to look as I sat at the kitchen table, a wealth of household tasks had been left half-finished. Frankly, I was surprised that Jago — who turned out to be as slight from the front as I'd observed him being from the back — had managed to complete the entire tea-brewing process. I couldn't help noticing, however, that where he had taken his tea with milk and sugar at the Vicarage, he had neither during our discussion. I asked him about it.

"I just ran out," he replied with a gormless grin. "I'm that hopeless sort of bachelor you read about in women's magazines." I wondered whether Elspeth wasn't the sort of woman who would put some order into his life. Probably too late for him to make a romantic gesture now, though — she'd been about to return to Boston on the day of the murder and would be delayed only a few more days.

I had failed to notice that Jago had been talking to me as I considered all this — extremely inconsiderate of him to butt in on a lady's private reverie, I'd say.

"Hmm?" I queried.

"I said what was it you wanted to ask me, Miss Caine?"

"Oh, that. Did you poison the Reverend Parbold?"

The cup quivered in his hand and a little of the dark brew splashed onto the saucer below.

"Quite direct, aren't you?" he asked with a nervous laugh.

"Yes. Did you?"

"No, why on Earth should I?"

"Perhaps because he was responsible for your father's suicide?"

Jago shook his head vigorously, as though battling some harsh interrogation or inner conflict. "I — I don't know that for certain. I mean, I never saw the note. Mother burned it."

"And where is your mother?"

"She died in 1925. It's just me now. And the echoes."

And the unfinished chores, I thought. Could a man incapable of completing a simple task like painting the banisters have the staying power required to commit a murder? And not your common or garden stab-in-the back either, but a clever and horrible poisoning? Frankly, I hadn't the faintest idea. The psychology of the individual, as the Belgian likes to call it, has never been my strongest suit.

Once again, I realised that Jago Meridian had been inconsiderate enough to be talking while I was thinking. Luckily, I was able to tell from his rather obvious mime that he was offering me a cup of tea.

"No," I replied, bluntly. Very bluntly, now I come to think of it; not even a thank-you. How rude.

"You surely don't think it's poisoned?" Jago responded.

"Is it?" I asked.

He put the cup to his lips and made a big show of swallowing a mouthful. "Delicious. Care for a cup?"

"No. Did you ever at least *think* about killing the vicar?"

"How is it going to sound if I say 'yes'?"

"I rather think you just did." Quite a sharp response, that. Clearly, I was on form that day.

"I thought about it every day of my life, Miss Caine. Every day. And every day I did nothing about it."

I wondered whether he'd ever read *Hamlet*. If he hadn't, I could have assured him that he wasn't missing much. But that's another matter entirely — did I ever tell you about the killing at Chandler's Block in Devon? I didn't? Oh well, another time, then.

"Tell me about that last day," I asked. "What went on at the luncheon; what was said and by whom."

Jago frowned. "Well, we talked about you, Miss Caine. I mean, what else was there to talk about? The Colonel's arrest was the biggest thing to happen in Overdale since — well, *ever*. Claude — Mr Mountjoy — described you as a colossal brain and a trim ankle. Then Elspeth said — well, that's not important."

"I'd like to hear it all the same," I said.

"She said, 'I haven't actually seen her, but from what I hear, her ankles aren't as trim as all that.' Sorry. Americans are rather forthright, aren't they? All the same, Mr Parbold chided her for it.

"Claude asked what I thought. I had seen you about the town, but he called it 'admiring the Goddess from afar.' He, er, he asked me to estimate the circumference of your ankles."

I smiled. At least, I smile whenever I think about it now, so I suppose I must have smiled then, also.

"The only reason I mention it at all," he continued, "is because of what happened next. I don't know whether you've heard this, but Claude couldn't resist baiting Mr Parbold, and that part of the conversation provided him with the perfect opportunity. The moment I saw the corners of his lips twitch, I knew he was going to say something provocative. 'You know, now I think about it,' Claude said, 'she has all the qualifications to be an actual goddess. All-seeing, all-knowing . . . the only difference between Miss Caine and the popular Christian deity is that *she* exists, whereas the figure we popularly refer to as —'

"Well, as you can imagine, Mr Parbold wasn't going to put up with this sort of talk at the Vicarage. *'That is enough!'* he raged. He apologised to Elspeth for raising his voice, but he stood his ground nonetheless. Claude was highly amused, of course," said Jago. " 'I would have thought the good Lord was big enough and old enough to look after himself,' Claude said. 'Apparently, I was mistaken. How blind I've been.' Well, the old man was almost apoplectic by this stage, which only gave Claude the opportunity to mock him further. 'A touch of indigestion? Perhaps you're finally finding your own words hard to swallow?'

"When it became clear that something was wrong, it was . . . well, it was all very strange. Claude was confused, hopelessly lost. Well, he would be, wouldn't he? Elspeth had to tell me at least three times to fetch the doctor. I just sat there, frozen . . . just watching him, until at last he was dead. I still don't know how I feel about it. Should I be happy? Relieved? Scared? I'm just — empty inside. That's everything that I can remember, at any rate. Is any of it of use?"

"I have absolutely no idea," I confessed, "but thank you, anyway, Mr Meridian."

"Call me Jago," he said, flashing me a winning smile of which I would not have thought him capable.

It wasn't until I was on my way back to Troughton's home that I realised that I'd forgotten to ask Jago why he hadn't eaten any sandwiches that fateful day. I made a mental note to stop making mental notes and start making actual notes instead. There was no tremendous mystery behind it, in any case. If you found yourself invited to dine with the man who caroused with your mother and hastened your father to his grave, would you have much of an appetite? Really, the luncheon was the worst of all possible worlds, so far as Parbold would have been concerned: on one side, the resentments of Jago Meridian, a young man who's confessed to fantasizing about murder, on the other, Claude Mountjoy, whose existence seems to have been given over to tormenting the late clergyman. I thought I'd at least worked out the method of poisoning, but I also had a suspicion that I was overlooking something fearfully obvious. What had I been thinking of when that half-notion had begun to bother me? Troughton, it seemed, had taken himself off to who knew where for who knew what purpose — I found it hard to imagine that it could be police work. So I settled myself down in his armchair and started to read my latest adventure. After a few paragraphs, I felt one of my tension headaches coming on. The depiction of Hilary Caine, Girl Detective in *Tittle Tattle* was about as far from reality as . . . well, I'm in danger of repeating myself on that point, aren't I?

So I decided instead to close my eyes and count my blessings, which included at that time the fact that I hadn't heard from my father in at least two years. As for my life as a semifictional detective, it wasn't all bad. I had the opportunity to travel, and I also had funds for the time being. And unlike Holmes, I didn't have to bother about my client because I could get on very nicely without a client, thank you very much. Of course, life was easier still for the Wimseys and the Poirots of this world. Despite the fact that the Belgian claimed to be a private detective, both men seemed to trip over corpses wherever they went, which struck me as extremely poor judgement on someone's part. I could never be that fortunate — except on this particular occasion, of course. But that was neither here nor there . . . wasn't it?

"Comfortable, Miss Caine?"

"Delightfully so, Inspector. I take it I've been asleep?"

"With a big beaming smile on your face," Troughton replied.

"Hardly surprising," I replied. "I'm in a good mood, and I doubt if anything could spoil it."

"Not even this?" He held out a piece of paper. "It arrived at the station half an hour ago. I went over there to see it for myself. Looks like your theories have come to nothing."

I read the telegram and laughed. "Don't you believe it. As a matter of fact, I think I'm ready to confront our merry band of suspects. The Vicarage would be an appropriate venue, don't you think? You see, I've finally discovered that all-important clue I've been searching for."

Troughton was unperturbed by my revelation. "Care to let me in on it, Miss Caine?"

I took great satisfaction in replying, "Sorry, Inspector, holiday's over. But I will say this: that clue has been staring you in the face all this time."

IT was another beautiful day. I waited as Elspeth Seagrave, Claude Mountjoy, and Jago Meridian were seated around the dining room table for the first time since the murder of Alistair Parbold. The young people were in no mood for conversation. Mountjoy, of course, could not be silenced.

"I say, Elspeth, this is wonderfully exciting, isn't it? I hope *I* turn out to be the murderer. I'm always hungry for fresh sensation."

"Claude, don't joke," said Elspeth, wearily.

"Gentlemen, Miss Seagrave," I said at last. "Thank you for coming to the Vicarage today."

Of course, none of them had really had a choice in the matter; Inspector Troughton can be quite persuasive when given sufficient encouragement. Now, however, he was quite happy in his usual position, slouched against a wall, simply observing proceedings.

"I don't want to inconvenience all but one of you more than necessary, so I'll get this over with as soon as possible. On the day Alistair Parbold was murdered, I was sure I'd identified the method by which he was poisoned. After all, he was the only person to take lemon with his tea."

For a moment, no one spoke. Then, Elspeth asked, "So the poison was in the lemon?"

"Oh, it's really very simple. Just inject it with a hypodermic and Bob's your uncle."

Mountjoy inserted a finger in his ear and began an excavation. "I don't see how that helps you, Miss Caine. I mean, any one of us could have done it."

"In fact, it helps us less than that, Mr Mountjoy." I displayed the telegram for the benefit of his two friends. "It turns out that my suspicions were incorrect. The poison was not in the lemon. Then I realised I'd been looking in the wrong place entirely. Fortunately, I drew up a list of everyone's lunchtime consumptions on the day of the murder, and it's quite obvious that the poison could have been nowhere else but in the teapot."

For a longer moment, no one spoke.

"But we all drank the tea, Miss Caine," Mountjoy pointed out. "Surely we'd all be dead."

"Too true, Claude. In fact, the only way the three of you could have been immune to its effects would have been if you'd all taken the antidote almost immediately. You all took milk in your tea, didn't you?"

For an even longer . . . oh well, you get the idea.

"The milk?" repeated Elspeth.

"The milk. You, Elspeth, never touch sugar, so that only leaves the milk, which you all had with your tea, except the victim. I've investigated a dozen poisoning cases, but I have to admit this one is quite unique. The murderer should take some pride in that."

Troughton — who, true to form, had remained silent in the background — spoke up at last. "But which of them *is* the murderer, Miss Caine? As far as I can see, it could still be any one of them."

"Well, that should have been obvious from the start, Inspector, but the identification of the guilty party hinges on one important factor. Remember, I told you it was staring you in the face from the beginning. Unfortunately, it only stared me in the face when I looked in a mirror."

"Are you confessing, Miss Caine?"

I chuckled. "Not hardly. But for the first time ever, I find that I'm the vital clue in one of my own investigations. Miss Seagrave, what was the principal topic of conversation during the luncheon?"

"Conversation?" she repeated. She was doing that a lot today. "Well, it was . . . *you,* Miss Caine. I mean, your presence here in Overdale, the way you solved that other case. You have quite a reputation."

Ordinarily, modesty would forbid, but in this instance, it was quite unavoidable, so I was forced to agree with her.

"Ask yourselves, if you were planning to commit a murder, would you do it when you knew for a fact that a celebrated detective was in the vicinity at that moment? Mr Mountjoy, you and the late Reverend Parbold were involved in an internecine conflict for years. You could have done him in whenever you wanted."

Mountjoy began to protest, but I had no time or patience for his "poor, helpless old blind man" speech, so I pressed on.

"You, Mr Meridian, you'd thought about killing the vicar since you were a boy." Jago was clearly extremely unhappy at my speaking this truth out loud, but there was no stopping me now. "Couldn't you have waited another week? Of course you could. No, the only reason for anyone to have killed Alistair Parbold on that particular day is because they knew it was going to be their last chance. Say, if they were about to leave the country?"

Elspeth goggled. She opened her mouth but nothing beyond a slight choking noise came out. At long last, she managed to say something that wasn't simply what I'd just said.

"Oh, Hilary, you are so wrong!"

"You assured us that you didn't know about your uncle's money, but I think you knew *all* about it."

"But I didn't! Not until he told me!" She waved a finger in Troughton's direction.

"So this is all just about money?" asked the Inspector, sounding a trifle disappointed.

"Yes, but the guest list for the luncheon served as an excellent distraction. What are the odds that two such excellent suspects should be on hand on the very day the Reverend is murdered? Probably as high as the odds that I should be on hand to solve it. And once you'd acquired the poison, Elspeth, it was just a matter of time 'til you used it. When you finally had to return to America, you decided: 'Hang the risk, I'm going to do it!' Isn't that how it happened? Unfortunately, the risk just hanged *you.*"

Troughton evidently viewed these words as his cue to act. He moved silently across the room and took Elspeth gently by the hand. She didn't struggle, but she was not happy.

"You think you know me?" she asked in a tone I had not heard her adopt before. "You don't know a thing about me."

"I know this much," I replied. "I don't think we're going to be friends after all."

The Musgrave Ritual

by Sir Arthur Conan Doyle

AN anomaly which often struck me in the character of my friend Sherlock Holmes was that, although in his methods of thought he was the neatest and most methodical of mankind, and although also he affected a certain quiet primness of dress, he was none the less in his personal habits one of the most untidy men that ever drove a fellow-lodger to distraction. Not that I am in the least conventional in that respect myself. The rough-and-tumble work in Afghanistan, coming on the top of natural Bohemianism of disposition, has made me rather more lax than befits a medical man. But with me there is a limit, and when I find a man who keeps his cigars in the coal-scuttle, his tobacco in the toe end of a Persian slipper, and his unanswered correspondence transfixed by a jack-knife into the very centre of his wooden mantelpiece, then I begin to give myself virtuous airs. I have always held, too, that pistol practice should be distinctly an open-air pastime; and when Holmes, in one of his queer humours, would sit in an armchair with his hair-trigger and a hundred Boxer cartridges and proceed to adorn the opposite wall with a patriotic V.R. done in bullet-pocks, I felt strongly that neither the atmosphere nor the appearance of our room was improved by it.

Our chambers were always full of chemicals and of criminal relics which had a way of wandering into unlikely positions, and of turning up in the butter-dish or in even less desirable places. But his papers were my great crux. He had a horror of destroying documents, especially those which were connected with his past cases, and yet it was only once in every year or two that he would muster energy to docket and arrange them; for, as I have mentioned somewhere in these incoherent memoirs, the outbursts of passionate energy when he performed the remarkable feats with which his name is associated were followed by reactions of lethargy during which he would lie about with his violin and his books, hardly moving save from the sofa to the table. Thus month after month his papers accumulated until every corner of the room was stacked with bundles of manuscript which were on no account to be burned, and which could not be put away save by their owner. One winter's night, as we sat together by the fire, I ventured to suggest to him that, as he had finished pasting extracts into his commonplace book, he might employ the next two hours in making our room a little more habitable. He could not deny the justice of my request, so with a rather rueful face he went off to his bedroom, from which he returned presently pulling a large tin box behind him. This he placed in the middle of the floor, and, squatting down upon a stool in front of it, he threw back the lid. I could see that it was already a third full of bundles of paper tied up with red tape into separate packages.

"There are cases enough here, Watson," said he, looking at me with mischievous eyes. "I think that if you knew all that I had in this box you would ask me to pull some out instead of putting others in."

"These are the records of your early work, then?" I asked. "I have often wished that I had notes of those cases."

"Yes, my boy, these were all done prematurely before my biographer had come to glorify me." He lifted bundle after bundle in a tender, caressing sort of way. "They are not all successes, Watson," said he. "But there are some pretty little problems among them. Here's the record of the Tarleton murders, and the case of Vamberry, the wine merchant, and the adventure of the old Russian woman, and the singular affair of the aluminum crutch, as well as a full account of Ricoletti of the club-foot, and his abominable wife. And here — ah — now this really is something a little recherché."

He dived his arm down to the bottom of the chest and brought up a small wooden box with a sliding lid such as children's toys are kept in. From within he produced a crumpled piece of paper, an old-fashioned brass key, a peg of wood with a ball of string attached to it, and three rusty old discs of metal.

"Well, my boy, what do you make of this lot?" he asked, smiling at my expression.

"It is a curious collection."

"Very curious, and the story that hangs round it will strike you as being more curious still."

"These relics have a history, then?"

"So much so that they are history."

"What do you mean by that?"

Sherlock Holmes picked them up one by one and laid them along the edge of the table. Then he reseated himself in his chair and looked them over with a gleam of satisfaction in his eyes.

"These," said he, "are all that I have left to remind me of the adventure of the Musgrave Ritual."

I had heard him mention the case more than once, though I

had never been able to gather the details. "I should be so glad," said I, "if you would give me an account of it."

"And leave the litter as it is?" he cried mischievously. "Your tidiness won't bear much strain, after all, Watson. But I should be glad that you should add this case to your annals, for there are points in it which make it quite unique in the criminal records of this or, I believe, of any other country. A collection of my trifling achievements would certainly be incomplete which contained no account of this very singular business.

"You may remember how the affair of the *Gloria Scott,* and my conversation with the unhappy man whose fate I told you of, first turned my attention in the direction of the profession which has become my life's work. You see me now when my name has become known far and wide, and when I am generally recognized both by the public and by the official force as being a final court of appeal in doubtful cases. Even when you knew me first, at the time of the affair which you have commemorated in 'A Study in Scarlet,' I had already established a considerable, though not a very lucrative, connection. You can hardly realize, then, how difficult I found it at first, and how long I had to wait before I succeeded in making any headway.

"When I first came up to London I had rooms in Montague Street, just round the corner from the British Museum, and there I waited, filling in my too abundant leisure time by studying all those branches of science which might make me more efficient. Now and again cases came in my way, principally through the introduction of old fellow-students, for during my last years at the university there was a good deal of talk there about myself and my methods. The third of these cases was that of the Musgrave Ritual, and it is to the interest which was aroused by that singular chain of events, and the large issues which proved to be at stake, that I trace my first stride towards the position which I now hold.

"Reginald Musgrave had been in the same college as myself, and I had some slight acquaintance with him. He was not generally popular among the undergraduates, though it always seemed to me that what was set down as pride was really an attempt to cover extreme natural diffidence. In appearance he was a man of an exceedingly aristocratic type, thin, high-nosed, and large-eyed, with languid and yet courtly manners. He was indeed a scion of one of the very oldest families in the kingdom though his branch was a cadet one which had separated from the northern Musgraves some time in the sixteenth century and had established itself in western Sussex, where the Manor House of Hurlstone is perhaps the oldest inhabited building in the county. Something of his birth-place seemed to cling to the man, and I never looked at his pale, keen face or the poise of his head without associating him with grey archways and mullioned windows and all the venerable wreckage of a feudal keep. Once or twice we drifted into talk, and I can remember that more than once he expressed a keen interest in my methods of observation and inference.

"For four years I had seen nothing of him until one morning he walked into my room in Montague Street. He had changed little, was dressed like a young man of fashion — he was always a bit of a dandy — and preserved the same quiet, suave manner which had formerly distinguished him.

" 'How has all gone with you, Musgrave?' I asked after we had cordially shaken hands.

" 'You probably heard of my poor father's death,' said he; 'he was carried off about two years ago. Since then I have of course had the Hurlstone estate to manage, and as I am member for my district as well, my life has been a busy one. But I understand, Holmes, that you are turning to practical ends those powers with which you used to amaze us?'

" 'Yes,' said I, 'I have taken to living by my wits.'

" 'I am delighted to hear it, for your advice at present would be exceedingly valuable to me. We have had some very strange doings at Hurlstone, and the police have been able to throw no light upon the matter. It is really the most extraordinary and inexplicable business.'

"You can imagine with what eagerness I listened to him, Watson, for the very chance for which I had been panting during all those months of inaction seemed to have come within my reach. In my inmost heart I believed that I could succeed where others failed, and now I had the opportunity to test myself.

" 'Pray let me have the details,' I cried.

"Reginald Musgrave sat down opposite to me and lit the cigarette which I had pushed towards him.

" 'You must know,' said he, 'that though I am a bachelor, I have to keep up a considerable staff of servants at Hurlstone, for it is a rambling old place and takes a good deal of looking after. I preserve, too, and in the pheasant months I usually have a house-party, so that it would not do to be short-handed. Altogether there are eight maids, the cook, the butler, two foot-men, and a boy. The garden and the stables of course have a separate staff.

" 'Of these servants the one who had been longest in our service was Brunton, the butler. He was a young schoolmaster out of place when he was first taken up by my father, but he was a man of great energy and character, and he soon became quite invaluable in the household. He was a well-grown, handsome man, with a splendid forehead, and though he has been with us for twenty years he cannot be more than forty now. With his personal advantages and his extraordinary gifts — for he can speak several languages and play nearly every musical instrument — it is wonderful that he should have been satisfied so long in such a position, but I suppose that he was comfortable and lacked energy to make any change. The butler of Hurlstone is always a thing that is remembered by all who visit us.

" 'But this paragon has one fault. He is a bit of a Don Juan, and you can imagine that for a man like him it is not a very difficult part to play in a quiet country district. When he was married it was all right, but since he has been a widower we have had no end of trouble with him. A few months ago we were in hopes that he was about to settle down again, for he became engaged to Rachel Howells, our second housemaid; but he has thrown her over since then and taken up with Janet Tregellis, the daughter of the head game-keeper. Rachel — who is a very good girl, but of an excitable Welsh temperament — had a sharp touch of brain-fever and goes about the house now — or did until yesterday — like a black-eyed shadow of her former self. That was our first drama at Hurlstone; but a second one came to drive it from our minds, and it was prefaced by the disgrace and dismissal of butler Brunton.

" 'This was how it came about. I have said that the man was intelligent, and this very intelligence has caused his ruin, for it seems to have led to an insatiable curiosity about things which did not in the least concern him. I had no idea of the lengths to which this would carry him until the merest accident opened my eyes to it.

" 'I have said that the house is a rambling one. One day last week — on Thursday night, to be more exact — I found that I could not sleep, having foolishly taken a cup of strong café noir after my dinner. After struggling against it until two in the morning, I felt that it was quite hopeless, so I rose and lit the candle with the intention of continuing a novel which I was reading. The book, however, had been left in the billiard-room, so I pulled on my dressing-gown and started off to get it.

" 'In order to reach the billiard-room I had to descend a flight of stairs and then to cross the head of a passage which led to the library and the gun-room. You can imagine my surprise when, as I looked down this corridor. I saw a glimmer of light coming from the open door of the library. I had myself extinguished the lamp and closed the door before coming to bed. Naturally my first thought was of burglars. The corridors at Hurlstone have their walls largely decorated with trophies of old weapons. From one of these I picked a battle-axe, and then, leaving my candle behind me, I crept on tiptoe down the passage and peeped in at the open door.

" 'Brunton, the butler, was in the library. He was sitting fully dressed, in an easy-chair, with a slip of paper which looked like a map upon his knee, and his forehead sunk forward upon his hand in deep thought. I stood dumb with astonishment, watching him from the darkness. A small taper on the edge of the table shed a feeble light, which sufficed to show me that he was fully dressed. Suddenly, as I looked, he rose from his chair, and, walking over to a bureau at the side, he unlocked it and drew out one of the drawers. From this he took a paper, and, returning to his seat, he flattened it out beside the taper on the edge of the table and began to study it with minute attention. My indignation at this calm examination of our family documents overcame me so far that I took a step forward, and Brunton, looking up. saw me standing in the doorway. He sprang to his feet, his face turned livid with fear, and he thrust into his breast the chart-like paper which he had been originally studying.

" ' "So!" said I. "This is how you repay the trust which we have reposed in you. You will leave my service to-morrow."

" 'He bowed with the look of a man who is utterly crushed and slunk past me without a word. The taper was still on the table, and by its light I glanced to see what the paper was which Brunton had taken from the bureau. To my surprise it was nothing of any importance at all, but simply a copy of the questions and answers in the singular old observance called the Musgrave Ritual. It is a sort of ceremony peculiar to our family, which each Musgrave for centuries past has gone through on his coming of age — a thing of private interest, and perhaps of some little importance to the archaeologist, like our own blazonings and charges, but of no practical use whatever.'

" 'We had better come back to the paper afterwards,' said I.

" 'If you think it really necessary,' he answered with some hesitation. 'To continue my statement, however: I re-locked the bureau, using the key which Brunton had left, and I had turned to go when I was surprised to find that the butler had returned, and was standing before me.

" ' "Mr. Musgrave, sir," he cried in a voice which was hoarse with emotion, "I can't bear disgrace, sir. I've always been proud above my station in life, and disgrace would kill me. My blood will be on your head, sir — it will, indeed — if you drive me to despair. If you cannot keep me after what has passed, then for God's sake let me give you notice and leave in a month, as if of my own free will. I could stand that, Mr Musgrave, but not to be cast out before all the folk that I know so well."

" ' "You don't deserve much consideration, Brunton," I answered. "Your conduct has been most infamous. However, as you have been a long time in the family, I have no wish to bring public disgrace upon you. A month, however, is too long. Take yourself away in a week, and give what reason you like for going."

" ' "Only a week, sir?" he cried in a despairing voice. "A fortnight — say at least a fortnight!"

" ' "A week," I repeated, "and you may consider yourself to have been very leniently dealt with."

" 'He crept away, his face sunk upon his breast, like a broken man, while I put out the light and returned to my room.

" 'For two days after this Brunton was most assiduous in his attention to his duties. I made no allusion to what had passed and waited with some curiosity to see how he would cover his disgrace. On the third morning, however, he did not appear, as was his custom, after breakfast to receive my instructions for the day. As I left the dining-room I happened to meet Rachel Howells, the maid. I have told you that she had only recently recovered from an illness and was looking so wretchedly pale and wan that I remonstrated with her for being at work.

" ' "You should be in bed," I said. "Come back to your duties when you are stronger."

" 'She looked at me with so strange an expression that I began to suspect that her brain was affected.

" ' "I am strong enough, Mr. Musgrave," said she.

" ' "We will see what the doctor says," I answered. "You must stop work now, and when you go downstairs just say that I wish to see Brunton."

" ' "The butler is gone," said she.

" ' "Gone! Gone where?"

" ' "He is gone. No one has seen him. He is not in his room. Oh, yes, he is gone, he is gone!" She fell back against the wall with shriek after shriek of laughter, while I, horrified at this sudden hysterical attack, rushed to the bell to summon help. The girl was taken to her room, still screaming and sobbing, while I made inquiries about Brunton. There was no doubt about it that he had disappeared. His bed had not been slept in, he had been seen by no one since he had retired to his room the night before, and yet it was difficult to see how he could have left the house, as both windows and doors were found to be fastened in the morning. His clothes, his watch, and even his money were in his room, but the black suit which he usually wore was missing. His slippers, too, were gone, but his boots were left behind. Where then could butler Brunton have gone in the night, and what could have become of him now?

" 'Of course we searched the house from cellar to garret, but there was no trace of him. It is, as I have said, a labyrinth of an old house, especially the original wing, which is now practically uninhabited; but we ransacked every room and cellar without discovering the least sign of the missing man. It was incredible to me that he could have gone away leaving all his property behind him, and yet where could he be? I called in the local police, but without success. Rain had fallen on the night before, and we examined the lawn and the paths all round the house, but in vain. Matters were in this state, when a new development quite drew our attention away from the original mystery.

" 'For two days Rachel Howells had been so ill, sometimes delirious, sometimes hysterical, that a nurse had been employed to sit up with her at night. On the third night after Brunton's disappearance, the nurse, finding her patient sleeping nicely, had dropped into a nap in the armchair, when she woke in the early morning to find the bed empty, the window open, and no signs of the invalid. I was instantly aroused, and, with the two foot-men, started off at once in search of the missing girl. It was not difficult to tell the direction which she had taken, for, starting from under her window, we could follow her footmarks easily across the lawn to the edge of the mere, where they vanished close to the gravel path which leads out of the grounds. The lake there is eight feet deep, and you can imagine our feelings when we saw that the trail of the poor demented girl came to an end at the edge of it.

" 'Of course, we had the drags at once and set to work to recover the remains, but no trace of the body could we find. On the other hand, we brought to the surface an object of a most unexpected kind. It was a linen bag which contained within it a mass of old rusted and discoloured metal and several dull-coloured pieces of pebble or glass. This strange find was all that we could get from the mere, and, although we made every possible search and inquiry yesterday, we know nothing of the fate either of Rachel Howells or of Richard Brunton. The county police are at their wit's end, and I have come up to you as a last resource.'

"You can imagine, Watson, with what eagerness I listened to this extraordinary sequence of events, and endeavoured to piece them together, and to devise some common thread upon which they might all hang. The butler was gone. The maid was gone. The maid had loved the butler, but had afterwards had cause to hate him. She was of Welsh blood, fiery and passionate. She had been terribly excited immediately after his disappearance. She had flung into the lake a bag containing some curious contents. These were all factors which had to be taken into consideration, and yet none of them got quite to the heart of the matter. What was the starting-point of this chain of events? There lay the end of this tangled line.

" 'I must see that paper, Musgrave,' said I, 'which this butler of yours thought it worth his while to consult, even at the risk of the loss of his place.'

" 'It is rather an absurd business, this ritual of ours,' he answered. 'But it has at least the saving grace of antiquity to excuse it. I have a copy of the questions and answers here if you care to run your eye over them.'

"He handed me the very paper which I have here, Watson, and this is the strange catechism to which each Musgrave had to submit when he came to man's estate. I will read you the questions and answers as they stand.

" 'Whose was it?'
" 'His who is gone.'
" 'Who shall have it?'
" 'He who will come.'
" 'Where was the sun?'
" 'Over the oak.'
" 'Where was the shadow?'
" 'Under the elm.'
" 'How was it stepped?'
" 'North by ten and by ten, east by five and by five, south by two and by two, west by one and by one, and so under.'
" 'What shall we give for it?'
" 'All that is ours.'
" 'Why should we give it?'
" 'For the sake of the trust.'

" 'The original has no date, but is in the spelling of the middle of the seventeenth century,' remarked Musgrave. 'I am afraid, however, that it can be of little help to you in solving this mystery.'

" 'At least,' said I, 'it gives us another mystery, and one

which is even more interesting than the first. It may be that the solution of the one may prove to be the solution of the other. You will excuse me, Musgrave, if I say that your butler appears to me to have been a very clever man, and to have had a clearer insight than ten generations of his masters.'

" 'I hardly follow you,' said Musgrave. 'The paper seems to me to be of no practical importance.'

" 'But to me it seems immensely practical, and I fancy that Brunton took the same view. He had probably seen it before that night on which you caught him.'

" 'It is very possible. We took no pains to hide it.'

" 'He simply wished, I should imagine, to refresh his memory upon that last occasion. He had, as I understand, some sort of map or chart which he was comparing with the manuscript, and which he thrust into his pocket when you appeared.'

" 'That is true. But what could he have to do with this old family custom of ours, and what does this rigmarole mean?'

" 'I don't think that we should have much difficulty in determining that,' said I; 'with your permission we will take the first train down to Sussex and go a little more deeply into the matter upon the spot.'

"The same afternoon saw us both at Hurlstone. Possibly you have seen pictures and read descriptions of the famous old building, so I will confine my account of it to saying that it is built in the shape of an L, the long arm being the more modern portion, and the shorter the ancient nucleus from which the other has developed. Over the low, heavy-lintelled door, in the centre of this old part, is chiselled the date, 1607, but experts are agreed that the beams and stonework are really much older than this. The enormously thick walls and tiny windows of this part had in the last century driven the family into building the new wing, and the old one was used now as a storehouse and a cellar, when it was used at all. A splendid park with fine old timber surrounds the house, and the lake, to which my client. had referred, lay close to the avenue, about two hundred yards from the building.

"I was already firmly convinced, Watson, that there were not three separate mysteries here, but one only, and that if I could read the Musgrave Ritual aright I should hold in my hand the clue which would lead me to the truth concerning both the butler Brunton and the maid Howells. To that then I turned all my energies. Why should this servant be so anxious to master this old formula? Evidently because he saw something in it which had escaped all those generations of country squires, and from which he expected some personal advantage. What was it then, and how had it affected his fate?

"It was perfectly obvious to me, on reading the Ritual, that the measurements must refer to some spot to which the rest of the document alluded, and that if we could find that spot we should be in a fair way towards finding what the secret was which the old Musgraves had thought it necessary to embalm in so curious a fashion. There were two guides given us to start with, an oak and an elm. As to the oak there could be no question at all. Right in front of the house, upon the left-hand side of the drive, there stood a patriarch among oaks, one of the most magnificent trees that I have ever seen.

" 'That was there when your Ritual was drawn up,' said I as we drove past it.

" 'It was there at the Norman Conquest in all probability,' he answered. 'It has a girth of twenty-three feet.'

"Here was one of my fixed points secured.

" 'Have you any old elms?' I asked.

" 'There used to be a very old one over yonder, but it was struck by lightning ten years ago, and we cut down the stump.'

" 'You can see where it used to be?'

" 'Oh, yes.'

" 'There are no other elms?'

" 'No old ones, but plenty of beeches.'

" 'I should like to see where it grew.'

"We had driven up in a dog-cart, and my client led me away at once, without our entering the house, to the scar on the lawn where the elm had stood. It was nearly midway between the oak and the house. My investigation seemed to be progressing.

" 'I suppose it is impossible to find out how high the elm was?' I asked.

" 'I can give you it at once. It was sixty-four feet.'

" 'How do you come to know it?' I asked in surprise.

" 'When my old tutor used to give me an exercise in trigonometry, it always took the shape of measuring heights. When I was a lad I worked out every tree and building in the estate.'

"This was an unexpected piece of luck. My data were coming more quickly than I could have reasonably hoped.

" 'Tell me,' I asked, 'did your butler ever ask you such a question?'

"Reginald Musgrave looked at me in astonishment. 'Now that you call it to my mind,' he answered, 'Brunton did ask me about the height of the tree some months ago in connection with some little argument with the groom.'

"This was excellent news, Watson, for it showed me that I was on the right road. I looked up at the sun. It was low in the heavens, and I calculated that in less than an hour it would lie just above the topmost branches of the old oak. One condition mentioned in the Ritual would then be fulfilled. And the shadow of the elm must mean the farther end of the shadow, otherwise the trunk would have been chosen as the guide. I had, then, to find where the far end of the shadow would fall when the sun was just clear of the oak."

"That must have been difficult, Holmes, when the elm was no longer there."

"Well, at least I knew that if Brunton could do it, I could also. Besides, there was no real difficulty. I went with Musgrave to his study and whittled myself this peg, to which I tied this long string with a knot at each yard. Then I took two lengths of a fishing-rod, which came to just six feet, and I went back with my client to where the elm had been. The sun was just grazing the top of the oak. I fastened the rod on end, marked out the direction of the shadow, and measured it. It was nine feet in length.

"Of course the calculation now was a simple one. If a rod of six feet threw a shadow of nine, a tree of sixty-four feet would throw one of ninety-six, and the line of the one would of course be the line of the other. I measured out the distance, which brought me almost to the wall of the house, and I thrust a peg into the spot. You can imagine my exultation, Watson, when within two inches of my peg I saw a conical depression in the ground. I knew that it was the mark made by Brunton in his measurements, and that I was still upon his trail.

"From this starting-point I proceeded to step, having first taken the cardinal points by my pocket-compass. Ten steps with each foot took me along parallel with the wall of the house, and again I marked my spot with a peg. Then I carefully paced off five to the east and two to the south. It brought me to the very threshold of the old door. Two steps to the west meant now that I was to go two paces down the stone-flagged passage, and this was the place indicated by the Ritual.

"Never have I felt such a cold chill of disappointment, Watson. For a moment it seemed to me that there must be some radical mistake in my calculations. The setting sun shone full upon the passage floor, and I could see that the old, foot-worn grey stones with which it was paved were firmly cemented together, and had certainly not been moved for many a long year. Brunton had not been at work here. I tapped upon the floor, but it sounded the same all over, and there was no sign of any crack or crevice. But, fortunately, Musgrave, who had begun to appreciate the meaning of my proceedings, and who was now as excited as myself, took out his manuscript to check my calculations.

"'And under,' he cried. 'You have omitted the "and under."'"

"I had thought that it meant that we were to dig, but now, of course, I saw at once that I was wrong. 'There is a cellar under this then?' I cried.

"'Yes, and as old as the house. Down here, through this door.'

"We went down a winding stone stair, and my companion, striking a match, lit a large lantern which stood on a barrel in the corner. In an instant it was obvious that we had at last come upon the true place, and that we had not been the only people to visit the spot recently.

"It had been used for the storage of wood, but the billets, which had evidently been littered over the floor, were now piled at the sides, so as to leave a clear space in the middle. In this space lay a large and heavy flagstone with a rusted iron ring in the centre to which a thick shepherd's-check muffler was attached.

"'By Jove!' cried my client. 'That's Brunton's muffler. I have seen it on him and could swear to it. What has the villain been doing here?'

"At my suggestion, a couple of the county police were summoned to be present, and I then endeavoured to raise the stone by pulling on the cravat. I could only move it slightly, and it was with the aid of one of the constables that I succeeded at last in carrying it to one side. A black hole yawned beneath into which we all peered, while Musgrave, kneeling at the side, pushed down the lantern.

"A small chamber about seven feet deep and four feet square lay open to us. At one side of this was a squat, brass-bound wooden box, the lid of which was hinged upward, with this curious old-fashioned key projecting from the lock. It was furred outside by a thick layer of dust, and damp and worms had eaten through the wood, so that a crop of livid fungi was growing on the inside of it. Several discs of metal, old coins apparently, such as I hold here, were scattered over the bottom of the box, but it contained nothing else.

"At the moment, however, we had no thought for the old chest, for our eyes were riveted upon that which crouched beside it. It was the figure of a man, clad in a suit of black, who squatted down upon his hams with his forehead sunk upon the edge of the box and his two arms thrown out on each side of it.

The attitude had drawn all the stagnant blood to the face, and no man could have recognized that distorted liver-coloured countenance; but his height, his dress, and his hair were all sufficient to show my client, when we had drawn the body up, that it was indeed his missing butler. He had been dead some days, but there was no wound or bruise upon his person to show how he had met his dreadful end. When his body had been carried from the cellar we found ourselves still confronted with a problem which was almost as formidable as that with which we had started.

"I confess that so far, Watson, I had been disappointed in my investigation. I had reckoned upon solving the matter when once I had found the place referred to in the Ritual; but now I was there, and was apparently as far as ever from knowing what it was which the family had concealed with such elaborate precautions. It is true that I had thrown a light upon the fate of Brunton, but now I had to ascertain how that fate had come upon him, and what part had been played in the matter by the woman who had disappeared. I sat down upon a keg in the corner and thought the whole matter carefully over.

"You know my methods in such cases, Watson. I put myself in the man's place, and, having first gauged his intelligence, I try to imagine how I should myself have proceeded under the same circumstances. In this case the matter was simplified by Brunton's intelligence being quite first-rate, so that it was unnecessary to make any allowance for the personal equation, as the astronomers have dubbed it. He knew that something valuable was concealed. He had spotted the place. He found that the stone which covered it was just too heavy for a man to move unaided. What would he do next? He could not get help from outside, even if he had someone whom he could trust, without the unbarring of doors and considerable risk of detection. It was better, if he could, to have his helpmate inside the house. But whom could he ask? This girl had been devoted to him. A man always finds it hard to realize that he may have finally lost a woman's love, however badly he may have treated her. He would try by a few attentions to make his peace with the girl Howells, and then would engage her as his accomplice. Together they would come at night to the cellar, and their united force would suffice to raise the stone. So far I could follow their actions as if I had actually seen them.

"But for two of them, and one a woman, it must have been heavy work, the raising of that stone. A burly Sussex policeman and I had found it no light job. What would they do to assist them? Probably what I should have done myself. I rose and examined carefully the different billets of wood which were scattered round the floor. Almost at once I came upon what I expected. One piece, about three feet in length, had a very marked indentation at one end. while several were flattened at the sides as if they had been compressed by some considerable weight. Evidently, as they had dragged the stone up, they had thrust the chunks of wood into the chink until at last when the opening was large enough to crawl through, they would hold it open by a billet placed lengthwise, which might very well become indented at the lower end, since the whole weight of the stone would press it down on to the edge of this other slab. So far I was still on safe ground.

"And now how was I to proceed to reconstruct this midnight drama? Clearly, only one could fit into the hole, and that one was Brunton. The girl must have waited above. Brunton then unlocked the box, handed up the contents presumably — since they were not to be found — and then — and then what happened?

"What smouldering fire of vengeance had suddenly sprung into flame in this passionate Celtic woman's soul when she saw the man who had wronged her — wronged her, perhaps, far more than we suspected — in her power? Was it a chance that the wood had slipped and that the stone had shut Brunton into what had become his sepulchre? Had she only been guilty of silence as to his fate? Or had some sudden blow from her hand dashed the support away and sent the slab crashing down into its place? Be that as it might, I seemed to see that woman's figure still clutching at her treasure trove and flying wildly up the winding stair, with her ears ringing perhaps with the muffled screams from behind her and with the drumming of frenzied hands against the slab of stone which was choking her faithless lover's life out.

"Here was the secret of her blanched face, her shaken nerves, her peals of hysterical laughter on the next morning. But what had been in the box? What had she done with that? Of course, it must have been the old metal and pebbles which my client had dragged from the mere. She had thrown them in there at the first opportunity to remove the last trace of her crime.

"For twenty minutes I had sat motionless, thinking the matter out. Musgrave still stood with a very pale face, swinging his lantern and peering down into the hole.

" 'These are coins of Charles the First,' said he, holding out the few which had been in the box; 'you see we were right in fixing our date for the Ritual.'

" 'We may find something else of Charles the First,' I cried, as the probable meaning of the first two questions of the Ritual broke suddenly upon me. 'Let me see the contents of the bag which you fished from the mere.'

"We ascended to his study, and he laid the debris before me. I could understand his regarding it as of small importance when I looked at it, for the metal was almost black and the stones lustreless and dull. I rubbed one of them on my sleeve, however, and it glowed afterwards like a spark in the dark hollow of my hand. The metal work was in the form of a double ring, but it had been bent and twisted out of its original shape.

" 'You must bear in mind,' said I, 'that the royal party made head in England even after the death of the king, and that when they at last fled they probably left many of their most precious possessions buried behind them, with the intention of returning for them in more peaceful times.'

" 'My ancestor, Sir Ralph Musgrave, was a prominent cavalier and the right-hand man of Charles the Second in his wanderings,' said my friend.

" 'Ah, indeed!' I answered. 'Well now, I think that really should give us the last link that we wanted. I must congratulate you on coming into the possession, though in rather a tragic manner, of a relic which is of great intrinsic value, but of even greater importance as a historical curiosity.'

" 'What is it, then?' he gasped in astonishment.

" 'It is nothing less than the ancient crown of the kings of England.'

" 'The crown!'

" 'Precisely. Consider what the Ritual says. How does it run? "Whose was it?" "His who is gone." That was after the execution of Charles. Then, "Who shall have it?" "He who will come." That was Charles the Second, whose advent was already foreseen. There can, I think, be no doubt that this battered and shapeless diadem once encircled the brows of the royal Stuarts.'

" 'And how came it in the pond?'

" 'Ah, that is a question that will take some time to answer.' And with that I sketched out to him the whole long chain of surmise and of proof which I had constructed. The twilight had closed in and the moon was shining brightly in the sky before my narrative was finished.

" 'And how was it then that Charles did not get his crown when he returned?' asked Musgrave, pushing back the relic into its linen bag.

" 'Ah, there you lay your finger upon the one point which

we shall probably never be able to clear up. It is likely that the Musgrave who held the secret died in the interval, and by some oversight left this guide to his descendant without ex- plaining the meaning of it. From that day to this it has been handed down from father to son, until at last it came within reach of a man who tore its secret out of it and lost his life in the venture.'

"And that's the story of the Musgrave Ritual, Watson. They have the crown down at Hurlstone — though they had some legal bother and a considerable sum to pay before they were allowed to retain it. I am sure that if you mentioned my name they would be happy to show it to you. Of the woman nothing was ever heard, and the probability is that she got away out of England and carried herself and the memory of her crime to some land beyond the seas."

www.ingramcontent.com/pod-product-compliance
Lightning Source LLC
Chambersburg PA
CBHW050827180626
46814CB00004B/1503

SHERLOCK HOLMES
MYSTERY MAGAZINE
VOL. 6, NO. 4   Issue #19

" HER ASPHYXIATION IS NO MYSTERY
THE GIRDLE MAKER DID IT. "

Publisher: John Betancourt
Editor: Marvin Kaye
Non-fiction Editor: Carla Coupe
Assistant Editor: Steve Coupe

Sherlock Holmes Mystery Magazine is published by Wildside Press, LLC. Single copies: $10.00 + $3.00 postage. U.S. subscriptions: $59.95 (postage paid) for the next 6 issues in the U.S.A., from: Wildside Press LLC, Subscription Dept. 9710 Traville Gateway Dr., #234; Rockville MD 20850. International subscriptions: see our web site at www.wildsidepress.com. Available as an ebook through all major ebook etailers, or our web site, www.wildsidepress.com.